The TEACHER - THE TONY

By ALAN M

Published by AMPS - 001

First published in Great Britain in 2013 by
AMPS
11, Gibbs Close,
Little Melton,
Norfolk NR9 3NU

Printed in Great Britain by Swallowtail Limited
Of Drayton Industrial Park,
Norwich NR8 6RL

ISBN 978-0-9575285-0-5

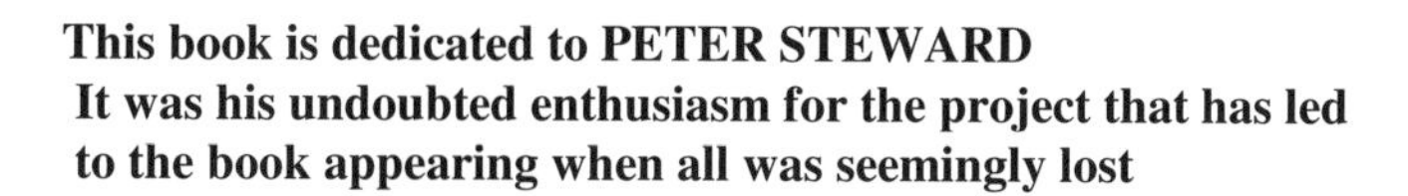
This book is dedicated to PETER STEWARD
It was his undoubted enthusiasm for the project that has led to the book appearing when all was seemingly lost

R I P The Teacher - 21st May, 1940 to 16th February, 2013

Illustrations from the collections of:
Alan Mann, Archant, Thorsten Knublauch
and with thanks to Roger Parsley, Anne Evans & the late Anna Sheridan

CONTENTS

INTRODUCTION

A bird does not sing because it has an answer,
It sings because it has a song. ***Chinese proverb.***

The story you are about to read is both a colourful and traumatic one. It details the life of my musician friend Tony McGinnity - Sheridan was his family name and the one he adopted for the stage from the moment he left home. We have known one another since our wartime Infant school days together in Norwich, through to the more recent years which finds him a widower, living alone in Seestermuhe, near Hamburg, in Germany, his main country of residence for much of his lifetime. The Schleswig-Holstein peninsula is a long way from his birthplace in England, in the heart of East Anglia. A fluent German speaker since the early 1960s, Tony must surely think of his adopted country as his spiritual home these days. You'll find as you read on that his life has been a kaleidoscopic and an almost surreal one, a life dedicated to music almost since its inception. In following this path a lot of 'heavy stuff' has ended up in his slipstream if we are to solely judge things by everyday standards.

Indeed, even the creation of the very book you are reading has been subject to an unexpectedly stormy passage and, until recently, it seemed unlikely it would ever appear in print. But it finally has, albeit in a modified way to what the author originally envisaged. To put it all in context, a potted timeline of the book's gestation follows and you'll see that it all began so promisingly back in 2006 when Tony and I routinely met up, again - as we often did - for a City of Norwich School (CNS) class reunion which I and my best pal John Sendall had as ever organised at a local hotel in Norwich . But it was to be a rather special reunion this time - 50 years having elapsed since our class of 5A (the Class of '56) had left school to face what was then a very different world.

I had not actually heard Tony sing in person since the '50s when I'd gone along to a gig in Norwich, this being just prior to his visits down to London and the 2 I's Coffee Bar and all of the skiffle/rock 'n' roll scene that was to follow. Now, for some reason, as this particular school reunion was drawing to its usual boozy conclusion, Tony asked if he could sing a few songs. I expected him to reprise a few upbeat standards from a bygone era. Instead, I and everybody present that night, were knocked out to find ourselves listening to a bunch of self-compositions, many quite introspective in nature, and a million miles away from the sort of fare he'd have churned out when he was briefly on our TV screens during the '50s, or later when he was in at the birth of the Hamburg scene. A scene incidentally that he helped to create for himself as Germany's adopted answer to Elvis Presley. Of course as we know, and it's been well documented in musical circles, the Beatles and many others were to famously follow the Hamburg trail in his wake. And there'll be much more about this using Tony's own evocative words to paint the picture. But one further point needs to be covered before we go on (a painful one as far as the author is concerned) which is to reveal just how the original book project came to be derailed at the eleventh hour and after such a promising start had been made.

(1) The Original Book Project - a Short Précis, 2006 onwards

Following on from that school reunion mentioned above, Tony and I chatted away on all manner of things and it was then that the possibility of a biography was first mooted. He, being aware that I'd written a book or two, seemed happy with my style and sympathetic stance towards music in general and was more than interested in a collaborative effort. He was quick to point out that he had no time at all for the scurrilous biographers and, without naming names, regarded the breed as *"repulsive and nasty in the extreme"*. But he was more than happy to talk about his childhood memories with someone who shared part of his upbringing. That appeared to mean me!

But he had to explain that he'd started his own autobiography a year or two earlier and, although this had temporarily stalled, he still had big hopes that he'd be able to get it completed at some future time with the help of his wife Anna. After returning to Germany he wrote to me in the July of 2006 and gave me the green light by saying: *"Alan let's envisage a biography as being the product of a mutual effort - make it happen, as it were, by active collaboration. If you're game, then so am I. Who knows, yours may turn out to be vastly better reading matter than my own effort"*. In fact much later he was to send me a photocopy of his aborted autobiography which amounted to only a chapter or two covering his very earliest years. Everything appeared to indicate that he was more than happy with the way our project was going. So far so good - or so it seemed at the time.

(2) Collaboration, with interruptions. (2006-2010)

In some ways the above years saw a fairly intensive period of collaboration, but it could also be fitful at times as Tony would suddenly find himself performing in parts of Scandinavia or else embarking on an extended trip to Mexico. This was no problem for me, a retired oldie whose music was his hobby and who was prepared to accommodate Tony's troubadour lifestyle with total forbearance if not a little envy! To get the bulk of his life-story ironed out it was agreed that I'd furnish him with around a 100 or so questions (via e-mail) but, because he didn't really like the electronic format - at this point his wife Anna acted as his secretary and expertly handled that part of his life - he suggested that he hand-write his answers which would then be faxed through to me. Of course I've carefully retained all of those sheets, after all Tony won prizes at school for his handwriting, and they are reproduced here verbatim, albeit in a printed format. Our text (mostly my questions, followed by his answers) are unaltered unless there was an obvious grammatical howler in evidence. These (thankfully) were fairly minimal, although the reader may feel several have been left in!

Of course the thrill for me, Tony's chum from way back when, was that he'd hopefully be both revealing and frank and, with both of us then approaching 70, there'd surely be very little that would be off-limits. There was one important caveat as the expression, *"Alan, my private life is sacrosanct"* was often repeated in a mantra-like way. I have to also confess that the e-mailed questions were put to him in a piecemeal, unordered way, so that, in an effort to make this present manuscript read coherently, I've had to juggle and sort things into some sort of loose chronological framework.

To continue, part way through the time span indicated above it became obvious that I'd have to visit with him and his late wife Anna to do a face to face question and answer session so as to supplement what Tony had already told me as well as clarifying several things he had written and which needed some explanation. And so it was that I eventually ended up as a guest in the 'Hobbit house' (their happy description) in Seestermuhe for several long sociable days, a delightful interlude that I'll never forget and which brings back many happy memories as I type this. (Bittersweet memories as his young wife Anna was to pass away so tragically early in 2011). But, to continue, it was around 2008/9 that an initial derailment - which was totally of my making- would arise, when, with the 50th anniversary of Buddy Holly's death looming, I was asked to do a new, revised edition of my A - Z of Holly's life with the welcome help of my publishers, Music Mentor books.

This was to bring about an enforced break in the 'Sheridan project', but Tony and I still kept in touch and in June 2010 it was their turn to leave the Boonies in Germany - as they usually termed it - and to stay with me and my wife in Norfolk. There were only a few minor queries to run by him at this juncture as well as getting his written consent to quote his song lyrics (which permission he graciously gave) and thus most of that visit was spent with my wife and I escorting them on a conducted tour of Norwich to see again the houses and locales where he had grown up and which obviously still meant such a lot to him. It was after this, and we're in 2011 by now, that the 85,000 word rough copy of the completed manuscript wended its way to my publisher for them to begin the daunting job of helping me knock the whole so-called project into some sort of publishable shape. I was always confident I could return to Tony to clear up any of mine or my publisher's queries.

(3) Project derailed (2011)

It's here that I have to reiterate that I was writing my friend's life story apparently with his complete co-operation, in an *as told to me* format (my italics), mainly because, to my knowledge, no such full-length Sheridan biography had ever appeared and his own autobiography had been long-promised but remained just that, an unfinished project. Furthermore, and if it doesn't seem too boastful, because we had grown up together, I was privy to the ins and outs of his early life - the pre-Beatles era - and I was thus well placed to get it all down. The reader also has to understand that in the past, many articles and even some books contained much in the way of disinformation where Tony's name was concerned. Simple examples will suffice: the alleged fact that he had been born in Cheltenham rather than in Norwich and the supposed fact that he had been fired off the TV pop show "Oh Boy!" by Jack Good and was virtually unemployable (it's said he lost the chance to appear on other similar shows) at the very instant he should have been most in demand. There was also very little learnt about his early years in Britain apart from the well known fact that, like so many of his contemporaries circa 1956-8, he'd come to prominence on the back of the Lonnie Donegan-fuelled Skiffle explosion. As implied earlier, our whole book project had, from the start, been agreed by no more than a handshake, and with no thought of any problems being envisaged. What on earth could go wrong? I can also recall Tony saying that my book would be for the British market while his would probably be for the German one.

It was in June 2011, while reading through a seemingly routine e-mail from Tony that he insisted on seeing a copy of the manuscript - or else. And I feel the need to quote his exact words, which were, as he termed it, not to use *"contentious material about living persons that is un-sourced or poorly sourced - potentially libellous or harmful to me appears."* Failure to comply, he wrote and, *"I shall be compelled to put the matter into the hands of a legal advisor"*. So for me that was really, dramatically that. I, for my part, felt left with little room for manoeuvre and felt that the green light for the project had suddenly gone straight from green to red. (And there's a Freudian slip included here readers, as ironically my friend Tony is quite literally colour blind!) He'd also said, and I'd written it down, *"Alan, there are no quotes I want to disown - if I said it I said it!"*

So, it suddenly seemed as if our lifetime relationship counted for nothing with this unexpected development: and believe it or not I also felt somewhat hurt as I'd never envisaged labelling my biography authorised. Indeed my greatest fear veered towards penning a book that would be a far too sanitised version of his life, more like a hagiography than a biography. Maybe it still is but I had always been determined not to sit in judgement of my friend, but instead, put out his story as far as possible using his own words, in order to bring his talent to a wider public. As to Tony's stance my publisher, a niche one who specialised in musical biographies and reference books, was now understandably disinclined to proceed with any sort of Sheridan biography with the fear of 'legals' hanging over us. And so that is how the original book project came to be mothballed for 12 months or more.

So what is it that has changed, and what is it that you're about to read? Well, it's certainly not the original book that hit the buffers. That manuscript remains with the original publisher gathering dust. But in recently re-reading all those replies he penned - and there must have been a 100 plus pages of stylish writings spread over those A4 sheets - I was convinced that Tony's life story should not simply end up in the recycling bin. It needed to be read even if it was destined to be a somewhat slimmed-down affair. And so, belatedly, here it is, with the word count at about two-thirds of the original text, but with Tony's words clearly used as quotations still comprising a substantial portion of the text. (In other words most of the 'missing' text comprised the musings of the author: perhaps not a bad idea.) However, I also needed to transcribe some of the answers from our face-to-face question and answer sessions, the one in Seestermuhe in Tony and Anna's home, and the later one in Norfolk, if the manuscript was to make any sense and not have big gaps in it. (Any content over and above each individual question and the answer which follows below, has been kept within reasonable bounds and added wherever some form of clarification is needed, or to help the reader place a particular answer within some sort of context.) Also, and to aid with the chronology, I've used a technique at the beginning of each chapter which I've labelled the **BACK-STORY** in an attempt to link up the whole into some sort of coherent framework. There's also a linking paragraph or two at the conclusion of each chapter.

I wrote to Tony to let him know that the revised book was coming out, and I firmly believe he can have little objection to such a development, given that he's given several extended interviews to journalists and suchlike over the years, even if most were heavily Beatles-related. He also sent me a copy of the lengthy interview he did with Genesis Publications (see Bibliography) back in 2002 and suggested I use this if it would help, and it was certainly useful to clarify certain aspects of his complicated life. So, in some ways does this book amount to just that, one more interview? Maybe it does. But - and it's a very big but - what follows is probably the most far-reaching interview and self-analysis that you're ever likely to get from this musical genius who it has been my pleasure to know for close to 70 years now. He remains a friend (well I hope so!) but he is without doubt both the most delightful and at the same time frustrating and enigmatic of individuals it has ever been my privilege to meet. I just hope the reader enjoys the ride and the extra insight it gives into his formative years in Britain, his search for a meaning to life and perhaps, most of all, into his relationship with The Beatles.

Of course it doesn't just end with the appearance of the Fab Four. He has also had the most amazingly topsy-turvy life since the '60s that would lead him to Vietnam (at the height of the war there) and his attempt thereafter to return to normality. The subsequent years have been spent pursuing his music in tandem with his own burning, spiritual quest, which continues to this day. To sum up, what we end up with might just throw some light onto what makes this enigmatic man tick and just why he still has such a passion to continue making music. He calls himself a troubadour and reminds me that he was, *"the first guy allowed to play electric guitar on British television"*. We know that in his time he was known as The Teacher to many musicians and, as such, he surely deserves more than ending up as a minor footnote in rock history.

(4) An Explanatory Note

Unless stated otherwise the punctuation and grammar, both his and mine, remains unaltered except for a few added sections (which covered our chats in Seestermuhe and to a much lesser extent back here.) His hand-written replies give you a great insight into his stylish manner, his quirky sense of humour and the off-beat way he often expresses himself: basically what makes him the man he is. As mentioned the format used throughout is this: author's question or query, followed by Tony Sheridan's answer, and finally the author's comments or clarification. To avoid repetition it was not felt necessary to place every one of his quotes within inverted commas but the author's words are italicised throughout so as to avoid any confusion between the interviewer/interviewee. Because Tony (who I also occasionally refer to as TS) has spent most of his life conversing in German sometimes his use of English and syntax is a little bit unusual (or at least, different to mine!) but it would not have felt right to alter much, if anything.

Finally, and leading with my chin at this point, I started off my lists of questions with some bravado, announcing: - *Tony I don't care how banal the questions are, I'm gonna ask them!* Some of the questions are indeed cringingly banal while some hardly qualify as questions at all but were posed in the hope of getting a response. And no doubt there are probably questions I should have asked but sadly didn't. But it's surprising to me just how much ground we managed to cover and what a fascinating insight it gives into his musical life and that of many of his contemporaries: read my blurb to the original book, below, and you'll get a taste of what is to follow. Thanks Tony, it was fun, and even if it was not all smooth sailing, it really was worth it. I hope the reader thinks so too.

BLURB TO THE ORIGINAL BOOK (2006)

...in the '50s he backed such artists as Conway Twitty and Brenda Lee having become the very first British artist to play an electric guitar on TV when appearing on "Oh Boy!"...he had to resist people in the business who wanted to market him as the 'British wild man of rock 'n' roll'...but he was good at resisting people...perhaps too good...

...then in the '60s he played some lead guitar with Gene Vincent and rhythm for Eddie Cochran who, it's known, could play a bit of guitar himself...soon he was in Hamburg acting as what Paul McCartney and others would term 'The Teacher' to The Beatles (who at that time were John, Paul, George, Stuart and Pete), whilst for a period Ringo Starr was his drummer before being recruited as part of the Fab Four...and that whole Hamburg and Beatles period is described here in his own vivid words ...soon Little Richard, Bill Haley, Cliff Richard and Jerry Lee Lewis would be among the many who were to call upon his instrumental talents...whilst he could sing a bit himself...

...then, after countless adventures (both tragic and hilarious) in Vietnam where he had gone to entertain the troops, he was reported in the musical press to have been killed... he wasn't, but he returned to Germany a very changed man...he may have been made an honorary Captain in the U.S. Army, but the music scene in the '70s was radically different and he himself wasn't the same man...seemingly down and out, in 1978 he was lured to America to front Elvis' TCB Band and a Las Vegas career beckoned only for the demons to return and another chance was blown...

...what follows thereafter is the story of the long trip that would have an unlikely start in rural Norfolk and continues to this day from his home in the Boonies (a rural idyll in the Schleswig-Holstein region of northern Germany) that he shares with his young wife Anna...a far cry from the broken war-torn home where it all started ...and a fractured personal life that would persist for years...

...so much had happened along the way...along a path that has seen him exploring the whole spectrum of musical sounds whilst developing a parallel search for a spiritual dimension to his life far removed from conventional religions...but we must first travel back to discover just how this tale has come about...in rock terms musical author Pete Frame calls him "The Hero of the Revolution" but he deserves to be remembered in his homeland as more than just a footnote in the history of The Beatles...his own story is unique but there's still more to come...

CHAPTER 1: A HEAVY SCENE - THE WAR-TORN YEARS

"Come up and see me when you are free,
Tell me your tale I'll listen,
Fill up a glass and spill your mind,
Talk of the times we're missing..."

This Time. Composer - Tony Sheridan

BACK-STORY: It all started out in another time, another era: Tony and I had both begun life as wartime babies, being born within six months of one-another in Norwich, the capital of Norfolk, deep in rural and insular East Anglia. (We probably didn't realise it then but travel a hundred or so miles in a more or less easterly direction out over the North Sea and you'd find yourself approaching the outskirts of Amsterdam: the then, for us, unknown Continent that would lure Tony was always close at hand.) As to the Norfolk capital itself, Norwich is an ancient municipality that for a brief time was England's second city behind London, having first appeared as Northwic on the coinage of Aethelstan the 1st of England, circa 920. It's said that from the year 1000 AD up to 1600, Norfolk was the most densely populated county in England, something it's hard to imagine in the 21st Century. These days Norwich the city, or Norfolk the county, don't hold many records although the former remains unchanged as the most easterly city in Britain. Enough of all that, it's at this point the questions need to start...

Question: *Were you born in Norwich or Cheltenham? (It seems some may have confused your name with that of Mike Sheridan.)*

Answer: I was born in NORWICH. Mike Sheridan may hail from Cheltenham. (Where the heck is Cheltenham, anyway?) An uncle of mine became Mayor of Chelmsford - but that's by the way...

Comments: *Mike Sheridan and the Nightriders were a minor outfit in the '60s who originated from the Midlands - they are listed as Birmingham Beatsters in Pete Frame's Rock Family Trees (see Bibliography) - and they were sometimes mistaken for Tony and his group, and vice-versa. The legendary Roy Wood was originally a member of the Nightriders and is on an early Columbia single of theirs. The question was posed to Tony (although the author already knew the correct answer) because the Encyclopaedia of Beatles People by Bill Harry had mistakenly listed Tony's place of birth as Cheltenham - a slip that has often been perpetuated by others.*

Question: *Please confirm your date of birth as 21st May, 1940. (Bearing in mind Joseph Murrell's classic Book of Golden Discs incorrectly lists your birth year as 1941).*

Answer: Confirmed: 21st May, 1940.

Comments: *Taurus on the cusp of Gemini is the way he termed it. And it was wartime and he'd put it this way in one of his song lyrics, "My soul felt sore, 'cause I was born in a war and revolution was on my mind..." . Strong words. And put another way I recall him using the phrase that, having been born in war-time, his "heart and his head were in conflict".*

Question: *Does the place and time of birth impact on one's life do you think? Did it for you?*

Answer: In retrospect all of past antics and meanderings, musical ups and downs, adventures and wanderings, encounters with danger and death, love and turmoil, doubt and depression, triumphs and losses, joys and passions, all reveal themselves as necessary and interlocking episodes. Quite literally 'one thing leads to another'.

Comment: *Of course whether or not the average person gives any credence to such astrological musings is debateable but his own life story does give us pause for thought. As will be revealed.*

Question: *Home birth, hospital or other?*

Answer: Born at home at 38, Glenmore Gardens, Norwich North. Must have been a difficult birth for Mum and me; as we were moved on doctor's orders to The Norfolk and Norwich Hospital. (Although I now feel that Mother shouldn't have later caused me to feel so guilty about having had such a bad time, stitches and all…).

Comment: *Because of the mention of the local hospital the author queried whether it really was a home birth. Response: "Absolutely 101% positive. (My information stems FROM my Birth certificate!"). Incidentally, this is the first mention (above) by Tony of the early trauma that followed on from his birth - the fact that the Second World War was underway, and the first air-raids on the City were about to occur, the first of 44 such raids in all, couldn't have helped.*

His birthplace in Glenmore Gardens (the house, No. 38, still stands) was in the north-west part of Norwich, and was in one of the areas badly damaged in such air raids as were two of the neighbourhood pubs, the Prospect House and the King Edward V11, either of which might have been for a time his father Alphonsus' local pub, although that's something we'll never be able to establish for sure.

Question: *Name of father please. Was he a Sheridan or a McGinnity?*

Answer: ALPHONSUS McGINNITY. His mother was nee Sheridan. His mother and other close relations (if, at all) spoke of my father as being "Irish through and through" - this said with various derogatory undertones. Their xenophobic attitude towards Germans, Japanese (and to a slightly lesser extent, Italians) was extended to include the Irish - more especially, Irishmen!

Comment: *The question of Tony's father's lineage, English or Irish - he was in fact born in England of Irish ancestry - is interesting. The author was surprised to learn, that Tony was no longer technically a British citizen at all but is described as Anthony Esmond O'Sheridan-MacGinnity (sic) on the only passport he possesses these days which is the one the Irish government issued to him during the 1970s. Quite why he revoked his British citizenship and claimed Irish citizenship is never really explained but seems to be a statement of fact.*

Question: *Mother's maiden name and do you know whether she was Jewish or partly so?*

Answer: Mother: Audrey Josephine Mary, nee MANN. Snippets of information heard when still quite small, but not forgotten, point to Mum's father (Josiah) as having been of Jewish descent. Mum's mother (nee BETTS) was a fervent Christian, so I presume that Josiah was either converted or "neutral". He was killed in France in World War One. (My Mum was born shortly after he died).

Comment: *You can imagine the author's amazement in learning that we shared the MANN surname, quite a co-incidence as we also lived only a street or two away from each other growing up and I did indeed have several other 'Mann' cousins who lived in neighbouring streets. Tony's mother came from London originally and our shared name is probably no more than a coincidence although my paternal grandmother's family also had London connections. So perhaps some extra research is needed!*

Incidentally, Tony's mother Audrey had been a highly accomplished musician herself, albeit as an amateur. Perhaps any progress she might have made was channelled instead into helping her obviously gifted eldest offspring. Certainly she became actively involved in tutoring him on a daily basis and was the driving force in pushing him on musically in those early years: she would be the person closest to home who tried, however bad his deteriorating behaviour was, to keep nurturing the musical spark that she knew lurked within her Anthony. But it was to lead to a head-on clash over musical styles that would prove to be a cause of ongoing friction between them, although encourage him she certainly did albeit in her ideal of classical music or, as she would term it 'proper music'. Their neighbours from those early days of the '40s and '50s (as explained below) can still recall the sounds emanating from next door's front parlour, with Audrey vigorously playing the piano and singing, whilst her young son joined in on his violin.

Question: *Where did you live during your 'Norwich years'?*

Answer: As you know I was born in 1940 in Norwich but from circa 1941 I lived in a children's home/clinic near Macclesfield, for several months at least. (This nearly killed me, no kidding!) Then from 1941/45 - various abodes, none of them fixed. One such sojourn was at a pub in Beccles (on the Suffolk border) called the "Waveney Inn". They had a grandfather-clock and it smelled of beer in wood casks. The landlord sported a Captain Hook-style wooden peg-leg and was extremely scary - but his wife was nice to me… Another strange stay was with a lady called Mrs. Rayner or Rainer, somewhere in the Norfolk countryside. Her place smelled of old-fashioned oil lamps. One day, I'll look these places up and maybe take drastic revenge!

Comment: *To remind readers this earliest period covered the Second World War. Tony's whereabouts during this period almost certainly reflected the domestic problems his mother experienced but he was never an evacuee as such. Norwich (and the surrounding area) although under attack - 1940/43 - did not officially evacuate its children. Rather children, like their parents, undertook gas mask drills, used *Anderson or *Morrison Shelters, etc and generally experienced the full terrors of war, situated as we are in the extreme east of the country.*

After the war, and back in the family home Tony and his mother and stepfather lived at the following houses and (as we'll discover) with a growing number of siblings:

(a) 1945 - approx 1953 , York Street, off Unthank Road, Norwich

(b) 1953 - 1958/9, Hansell Road, Thorpe St Andrew, Norwich. Thorpe was a village in Tony's day but it has been designated a Town in recent times, complete with a

mayor. Tony has never lived in Britain since the 1950s - his visits back have all been fleeting.

**Footnote:* Anderson Shelters (sometimes termed bomb shelters) were usually below ground and designed to protect anyone from air raids, whereas Morrison Shelters were cage-like constructions, most often placed indoors under a table, by families who didn't have access to a cellar, or an Anderson Shelter.

Question: *What are your main influences via father, i.e. genetically?*

Answer: Having Irish blood and playing modern music is a subject worth some closer scrutiny. Maybe it's mainly a question of temperament. There'd be no Beatles (and many others) without the Irish connection. Think of all the others, too. It's a long list... Hearing American music when quite young in years sort of conditioned the mind to receive what was to ensue after "Blackboard Jungle".

At home, mum played (only classical) piano and sang (contralto!). Little Anthony was sent to a lady tutor (Elsie Edmunds) down in the Cathedral Close in order to play the violin. That was some strenuous stuff, oh wow! Mum wanted me to blossom into a Yehudi (Menuhin) - or else become a vicar! When I was 15 or so, she just didn't want to understand that I NEEDED A GUITAR - BADLY! Oh, well.

Comment: *The Irish influences touched on above are turned to as a theme in much greater detail later on. The Blackboard Jungle film of 1955 starring Glenn Ford and Sidney Poitier, featuring Bill Haley's "Rock Around the Clock" as an occasional backdrop, made a huge impact both in Britain and America when it was first released.*

Question: *Some time later, I followed up the above question by asking Tony to elaborate on the question of being in a Children's Home during the early war years and he firstly recalled the horror of being taken there. Later he would vividly recall having "poor legs" and needing special boots to support himself.*

Answer: We had made the journey by train from Norwich to Macclesfield. The next thing I realise I'm standing in a cot with railings, screaming insanely, incredulous at the gradual fadeout of my mother's figure diminishing into the distance. *Prompted further he explained:* the childhood trauma of the kid's home/clinic near Macclesfield (near Liverpool!!!) has never left me. I'd be grateful for any authentic news on the "why/how of it" pertaining to those days. Think I nearly died in that place. When one considers that one's earliest memories begin around three, it's sort of spooky and horrific to recall those impressions - I was one plus years old!

The childhood trauma of the children's home near Macclesfield never left me...this period nearly killed me...no kidding! One day, my mother arrived to take me home. To portray the feelings of utter joy her appearance released in my wretched child's heart defies description. Attempting to write about my very earliest memories is to stir up buckets of excruciating laming emotions. Poor mum, what a shock it must have been for her when she saw what had become of me. God bless her. It must have been an awful picture.

Comment: *Tony appears to have tracked down the home (long since gone) to a point mid-way between Macclesfield and Bollington in the north of England. An Ordnance survey map shows a Swanscoe Hall, which may well have been the source of* *those indelible memories.*

Question: *Details of father's departure from your life and was this permanent? (Author: this provoked an extremely lengthy reply from Tony, but it's felt necessary to quote it in full as it gives quite a penetrating insight into his early years).*

Answer: My brother Stephen was born 23rd April, 1942. At some date prior to Steve's birth, my parents separated. The only time in my childhood I recall ever having even seen my father, was at Norwich Shire Hall when their divorce was finalised. When the judge eyed me sternly and asked if I should be given into the care and protection of my father, I just screamed blue murder until the QC decreed that I should be allowed to stay with my mother. I must have been aged three or four at the time. It took me years to get over the shock I experienced at those proceedings.

My mother was decidedly 'low church', viz Baptist, Methodist, occasionally Salvation Army. However, my father was a devout Roman Catholic. This led to their church marriage ceremony having been performed in a church of 'neutral' denomination, i.e. Prince's Street Congregational Church, in Norwich. Not so when it comes to the question of my Baptism! With the malediction of the Church of Rome and the fear of holy retribution lurking around the next corner, he insisted that I be baptised in St. John the Baptist (sic!) RC Church! Which I was!

The schism that eventually led to my parents' separation was fuelled by religious and racial, and age differences prejudices. He was almost 20 years her senior and already twice divorced when they met!

Their initial meeting had a poignant quality about it: at that time (early 1939?) my father was employed at the Telephone Exchange as an operator. Mum, looking for a particular connection, happened to encounter "my father's voice" as it were. One phrase lead to another, and they arranged to meet in the grounds of Norwich Castle. "He had a lovely speaking voice..." she used to say.

Mum's relatives were against the union from the start. Had her mother still been living, the opposition to their marriage would probably have been an insurmountable obstacle. (Guess my parents had to be brought together "by hook or by crook". Things had to fall together, as the Germans say with their word: ZUFALL(EN) which has no apt translation except perhaps "co-incidence", which in English implies "chance" or "luck". C. G. Jung's word/theory "synchronicity" is closer, and implies the existence of a higher, and more metaphysical, interpretation i.e. that all events at a particular point in time are related and meaningful if understood esoterically.)

Comment: *There's a lot of Tony's inner world coming to the fore in that revealing and searingly honest reply. Incidentally it was also a joy to both of us that we found we had so many shared passions in life - the writings of C G Jung, who believed in the "synchronistic connective principle" - which adorn my bookshelf, and his, being the first of many such happy coincidences. Incidentally, talking later he felt that it was probably his father's second marriage, and not his third.*

When at long last he did eventually rejoin his mother and brother it was to find that peace had finally broken out throughout the land, landing him with a new parent, a stepfather named Jimmy Guymer, who was actually a man from out of his mother's past. It would be nice to think that the story from now on gets noticeably better but sadly this was not to be the case.

Question: *Is he (your father) still alive? I know mother died in 1971 and step-dad Jimmy Guymer 'some time' ago. More details if possible. (This question also evoked the most lengthy and detailed of replies, but again it's felt best to give his answer in full.)*

Answer: Born in 1900, he died sometime in the (his) eighties in Lowestoft. Having searched for his whereabouts, I discovered that he was again living in Norfolk, after having worked and lived in Cambridge and Ipswich. Our "first" meeting in 1975 found us in his local pub, exchanging life-histories. It was somehow gratifying to learn that - although most of his childhood had been spent with an aunt in Dublin - he had actually been born in...Liverpool, of all places! (West Derby to be exact). Most intriguing was his account of how he, aged 17, told the British Army recruiters that he was older, in order to join the army. His cavalry unit was shipped out to India for the remainder of the war.

He showed me a faded photo of himself taken in India, looking spruced and polished in his tropical riding gear and boots. It was not difficult to identify with this lively old gent - still tall and straight, with a wacky sense of humour, and charming, to boot. (In moments of desperation, when my behaviour became too much to handle, mum would shout: "You're a chip off the old block!" - whatever that was supposed to mean, like I was cursed with a myriad unforgivable traits, all of them macho, coarse and vulgar.) I'm a chip off the old block, alright.

Jimmy Guymer was a "Sprowston man" from Blue Boar Lane, which was named after the country pub at the nearby intersection, the "Blue Boar". Mum and he had been "courting" before she met my father.

Did I as a boy occasionally feel a twinge of guilt when considering that I was "only" Jimmy's stepson? Did he look at me and see my father's face reflected back by my otherness of appearance and attitude? Sometimes when he hit me, I certainly thought he almost wanted to kill me - he just didn't stop. Mum didn't (or couldn't) stop or restrain him - she just kept screaming: "Don't hit his head, not on his head!!!" I never forgave either of them for that kind of incident. Thankfully, it didn't happen often. Later, I swore that if I had children of my own, I would never raise a hand against them, ever - under no circumstances whatever.

And I kept my oath. But I did punish myself often enough - but that's another story altogether.

Comment: *To explain, Sprowston is really a part of Norwich but towards the outskirts and well outside the old medieval City walls. On a personal note (and another coincidence) the author's father, Salem, served in India from 1919 onwards, also in a cavalry unit, albeit a different one to Tony's biological father, Alphonsus. And (final co-incidence) both were boxing champions for their respective army regiments! Wouldn't it be kismet to think they had actually fought against one another out there in India?*

Question: *As a supplementary I asked him about the origin of his father's name, McGinnity.*

Answer: I was named Anthony (after a Saint Anthony) Esmond (after Esmond Knight a popular pre-war actor whom my father apparently closely resembled) and as a middle name, Sheridan, the name of my grandmother's family in Ireland. I have always assumed (and secretly hoped) that little Anthony was the product of a tempestuous, but deep 'coupling of two souls' as the dramatist Ben Johnson once wrote.

Comment: *As a creative artist Tony takes his ancestral name somewhat seriously and has researched his Irish roots probably with the heraldic aspect of it as an added incentive. To remind the reader our subject was* <u>*not*</u> *in fact Christened a Sheridan at all but had been born with the surname of his father, Alphonsus McGinnity. As to the McGinnity surname most genealogical directories show the surname as being frequently clustered around County Monaghan, in Ireland. Both Alphonsus' father and mother, Patrick and Rosa McGinnity, and his grandfather Michael were from County Donegal: each county sharing its borders with the six British counties in the North. The name of Sheridan is mostly linked with the neighbouring county of Cavan.*

Question: *I'll try and trace your brother Stephen. Were there other brothers and sisters?*

Answer: My brother Stephen (Guymer), born 1942. Two sisters: Cathy and Jane (Guymer). Another brother: Paul Guymer. All alive and well, somewhere in Norfolk, I guess (I hope).

Comment: *Tony asked the author to try and track down his brother Stephen from whom he was estranged at this time (circa 2006). I did eventually find him, a retired Prison Officer, living locally but in a conversation which didn't get beyond his front door-step - he made it very clear to me that he held strong feelings of resentment towards Tony, some of which he confided to me. The problems had surfaced again in 1971 following their mother's death, with Tony unable to get back for her funeral because of musical commitments in Berlin, a fact that didn't go down at all well. But he recalls "I cried for three days" and felt her loss quite desperately despite the fact that "she labelled rock 'n' roll as the work of the devil." But Tony also concedes that not everything was the fault of others and is quick to acknowledge that he was a handful both during his childhood and indeed throughout much of later life.*

Question: *Via the telephone, I asked for a bit more background on his 'parents' - especially his mother - and his estranged brother Stephen. He answered in writing (below) in a deeply analytical fashion and ended up reflecting on his wartime years.*

Answer: If my father's version is correct, then mother went down to London around August 1941, (presumably to visit Aunts Flo and Ethel) and returned pregnant with my brother. (Which he gave as the primary reason for their break-up. He said that <u>he</u> couldn't have been Steve's father.) He told me this in 1975, when he was 75 and I was 35. (Our first 'conscious' meeting!) My impression was that he was being truthful without showing bitterness - just relating the facts. I'd preferred not to hear - or believe - him. On the other hand all the pieces seemed to fit in. "All's fair in love and war" comes to mind. Steve never for a moment showed any interest in meeting "our" father, especially after I had told him of my father's version of things. (Maybe wrongly, I figured that Steve should hear the "truth" from me, rather than my father).

There is a photo of me, aged approximately 15 months with my Aunt Myrtle (Alice's daughter) taken at Kinghorn Road. Probably just prior to being sent off to

Macclesfield. At least that's what Myrtle's facial expression seems to express. I've often wondered who took the picture. Was that when my mother was visiting in Shepherds' Bush (or Acton) I recall both names coming up in conversations when I was just a toddler at Aunty Alice's place during the war, when the windows were darkened and the BBC Home Service was listened to by all those present. In those days I was (passively) smoking the equivalent of 2 or 3 cigarettes a day, mostly under the dining room table where I would be safe if the bombs came. When the air-raid sirens went off, however, everyone proceeded to the hole-in-the-ground bunker, located in the back garden. There was lots of noise in the sky and the searchlights swung about like long knives on a cutting spree. Warm in my blanket, in somebody's arms, I sensed the urgency of leaving the house for a very good reason, and felt safe and protected... and loved, too.

Much later, there were frantic reports of a "dud" bomb landing somewhere next door in somebody's potato patch. (*Lord Haw-Haw had, in one of his broadcasts from Berlin, predicted that the Luftwaffe would bomb certain areas (even certain streets) in Norwich - which they certainly did...). I distinctly remember the "da-da-da-dum" (Beethoven's Fifth) on the radio - and the voice of some enemy (Lord Haw-Haw?) repeating those two words "Germany calling, Germany calling". It was a trying time for the grown-ups - but I do not recall ever having been afraid in the sense that danger was imminent.

**Footnote:* Lord Haw Haw was the nickname for the British traitor, William Joyce (1900-1946), who broadcast Nazi propaganda to Britain during the second World War. He was subsequently executed for his crimes.

My own personal horror scenario was yet to come - and when it did, I was devastated and very nearly destroyed for good. The war produced countless emotional cripples - are we all still dealing with the late aftermath of our childhood experiences? It would certainly seem so. Psychologists currently report that men around 60+ are having to deal with lots of long-suppressed stuff resulting from adverse childhood events in areas directly affected by the "heavy end" of war. Seems that men typically deal with these traumas on a superficial level, whereas women approach the "emotional content" rather more successfully, not allowing it to become - as it were - a laming factor. Anyway, I've always secretly admired those kids who - despite the turmoil of war - retained a semblance of an intact family life, where love was never lacking. *(Author - he expands on this theme in a later answer.)*

Comment: *The "dud" bomb could very well have been in Norwich where air-raids were a feature from 1940 to 1943 and such lucky escapes were not uncommon. Tony also told the author of a surprisingly happy interlude spent in Kinghorn Road in Norwich, with a loving Aunt, Alice Betts ("I loved her more than I loved my mother"). It's clear that Tony, the eldest child of five living siblings (a set of twins, Jonathan and Mary, having died in early infancy) felt somewhat of an outsider among his expanded family. Tony is particularly sad when mention is made of those twins mentioning to the author that the cause of death was probably a simple infection that wouldn't be fatal these days.*

Question: *What junior school did you go to in Norwich? Does Cheltenham figure?*

Answer: Again - Cheltenham doesn't figure at all at any point in my younger days. When I was about five years old, my mum took me to the Bignold Infant School, which was attached to Bignold Primary which in turn had four pairs of consecutive classes, up to the so-called "11-plus" exam. There I spent at least six fairly pleasant years - except for the incident of me receiving "the cane" from the Headmaster, Mr. Baker!

During World War II and afterwards there was a shortage of younger teachers, especially men, who'd gone to war some of them never to return. Consequently some older pensioned teachers were brought back to life to fill the gaps. The ladies were all "Misses", whether older or younger - Miss Stone did us infants a great service by playing us records of classical cello pieces . She would invariably shed a tear or two during these early music lessons, and it occurred to some of us kids, I'm sure, that she was thinking of someone special whom she'd lost in the war... We wartime kids learned to recognise the signs of personal sadness, wherever we saw it. The war affected folks at all levels of society, of all ages, all occupations and... school life was no exception.

*Author - Tony then becomes very involved in looking at psychological aspects...*Alan, kids are sensitised by emotions, and shaped by (personal) tragedy, they intuitively feel compassion and are in empathy with those who are suffering. Not long ago, I read something in a psychological periodical, the gist of the article being that the war generation - that is, children born around 1940 and who are now in their middle sixties - i.e. "retiring" age: a hitherto unseen phenomenon (at least in this generation) is becoming increasingly evident, viz, suppressed post traumatic disorders, resulting from negative World War II experiences, are resurfacing, having never been "dealt with".

Comment: *The author also recalls being with Tony at the Bignold School Infants (familiarly known by its street locality, Crooks Place) for a couple of years, before we as a family moved away across town. A former classmate of ours, Roger Parsley, vividly remembers a particularly gross piece of behaviour on Tony's part. Here is his particular memory: "Rebellion always seemed to be his middle name. I remember we had a teacher of the 'old school' named Ma Tench. She and he had running battles and one cold January day I remember him upsetting her so much that she hit him over the head with a third-pint, half frozen milk bottle, pushed him out into the playground and then, as a kind of punctuation mark, threw his cap out of the window at him!"*

Not perhaps the sort of scenario we can visualise happening these days without subsequent litigation and indeed it's an incident that TS refused to confirm happened although one suspects that it did, even if the description has acquired a somewhat theatrical flourish in the retelling. Curiously the former schoolmate - Roger Parsley - who provided the above tale would himself form a Norwich skiffle group in the '50s with a name that was the very antithesis of The Saints, Tony's later skiffle group: they would literally be known as The Sinners! It's worth adding that the school buildings of the Bignold (now known as Bignold First School and Nursery) are still recognisable to any former pupils even if almost everything else in the locality looks radically different these days. Most of the area was demolished by German bombs, resulting in a landscape littered with temporary homes, prefabs as they were termed, for years to come.

Tony's lyrics are often self-descriptive and will occasionally be used during the course of his story, whether they scan or not poetically...

"Now sometimes on a Sunday, I've been known to kneel in prayer
To thank the Lord for what we got, and let him know I care,
Now I may be a sinner, but He sees things my way,
He's gonna let me off on a Monday - kinda like a holiday

Four Day Workin' Week. Composer - Tony Sheridan

...in the chapter which follows our story moves forward to our years at Senior (Grammar) school, from late 1951 to mid 1956, where we would once again find ourselves thrown together although, as will be seen, it wasn't until the second year of school that we found ourselves in the same 'middle' class of 2A. Maybe there's a little bit of destiny mixed in at this point. Having been separated whilst in junior school, when I'd moved miles across the City and ended up in a different Primary school, we now found ourselves thrown together in the same Grammar school and, by mid-1952, also back in the same classroom as well. I'm inclined to believe that there is a bit of fate involved, and perhaps Tony does too as, a while back, he (politely I hope) referred to me as his *"mirror image"*. Certainly his years in the CNS were to be much more eventful than mine and (musically speaking) he would achieve a great deal more, as you'll read...

CHAPTER 2: GRAMMAR SCHOOL KID - SKIFFLE GROUP KING

"Well I went down to play on a Saturday night
I said: 'Hey, Lonnie, give us half a light'
I feel like making some music on my beat-up ole guitar
When I was young"

When I Was Young. Composer - Tony Sheridan

BACK-STORY: Initially Tony tried manfully to conform to the constraints imposed by a uniform-wearing grammar school; namely, The City of Norwich School, situated in Eaton and known then and now by its initials, the CNS. (The school housed about 850 pupils when we joined: 50 years on, like so many others, it has become an Academy and sports almost double that number.) But the panacea for the young Anthony, as his mother would always call him, was that music, that silver thread, had at last begun to move centre stage as a precursor to taking over his life completely. There's no doubt at all that he was a highly gifted young man. Even during his very first year at senior school he was singled out to take one of the named parts in the annual Gilbert and Sullivan production (The Mikado in 1951) whilst at the same time he was soon tackling classical music in all of its varied forms, graduating eventually to first violin, and precociously leading the school orchestra.

And although his classroom behaviour hadn't noticeably improved, he found that his prowess as a musician meant that he was treated far more leniently than most of his fellow pupils. As a junior he'd been caned at the Bignold but here at the CNS he was to be initially cocooned by his obvious prowess as a classical musician, although it wouldn't be very long before he would seriously test the grudging goodwill of the stern Headmaster, the austere Mr Jackson (nicknamed Rupert by all), to the limit. Now back to those questions… although an admission is needed at this juncture and it's this. Because I was aware of most of Tony's activities whilst at the Senior school it seems that I didn't bother asking him many probing questions about this particular period in his life. So, there's a rather disproportionate amount of the author's input for the moment: but the reader needs to know what part the school played in Tony's life, albeit mostly in my words in the absence of his.

Question: *At senior school did you play in the Junior Orchestra under Mr. Skeens?*

Answer: I recall only one school orchestra, under Mr. Skeens. At one time I was the leader.

Comment: *Tony's right, my memory's wrong. I have all the old school magazines and mention is only made of the one orchestra - and they had a pretty wide repertoire ranging from Gilbert and Sullivan to Wagner. Tony played first violin.*

Question: *What actual classes were you in at the CNS? Was it 1C then 2A and then you dropped out and came back again? Can you remember more?*

Answer: I was in 1A, (Mr. Spruce, form master) along with David Linstead (*author - the latter was a mutual friend of both of us. But I was in 1B at this point, before* *moving to the middle A stream.)* All those geniuses!! Urgghh!! (Alan, I never dropped out and came back again! - you can check with the school. (*author - he did briefly, and it's shown in the school magazine to boot. One of the few instances of Tony's memory erring or perhaps being a trifle selective.)* In 1A I decided that (apart from art and music) my only claim to fame was going to be... winning the annual prize (book) for "handwriting"! Of course, I was not made for the "S" (for science) stream, but I might have done alright in the "L" (for Languages)!... Well, these days I speak perfect German (much better than class 2L could've provided), and later also developed something of an interest for Latin, history, heraldry and other learned subjects...(Surprisingly I did spend a boring term in the sixth-form before graduating to Art School, where they accepted me with open arms!). Opposite the Art School was (still is) a pub called the "Red Lion", where some of my most memorable early performances took place. (The majority of Art School creative activities also took place in the pub!).

Comment: *Despite being hard to handle during his later school years, and we'll hear more of his escapades, nevertheless Tony has exceptionally fond memories of those days because of the grounding he got in the arts and (proper) music. A minor footnote - both Tony and I studied Art together at the CNS and we both attained a pass in the GCE exam. Musically he was a soloist in the Madrigal Society and as mentioned actually led the school orchestra (as lead violinist) at some stage. (The Art School period only lasted a few months, and really there's not too much that needs to be said under that heading, apart from the fact that the pub is now The Dog House Bar, believe it or not, while the Arts school has re-invented itself as the Norwich University College of the Arts.)*

Question: *There was a Heraldry hobbies group at the CNS school - were you in it?*

Answer: Was there?

Comment: *A surprise answer. Heraldry is an absolute passion of Tony's and I was amazed he expressed ignorance of this. Probably his enthusiasm developed later - he was 100% music at this point. As he said to me on several occasions, "Alan, without music life would be unimaginably empty and devoid of meaning". Before we go on it's worth a few paragraphs to look at the school as it was back in those days:*

The CNS - our supposed seat of mutual learning!

As to the main school buildings, circa 1951, these came complete with acres of playing fields which contained literally enough room for six or so full-size football pitches (although Tony would opt for hockey), countless outbuildings whose main purpose involved housing the woodwork/metalwork classes, a gymnasium, some immense cycle sheds, a tuck shop and a pair of fives courts, and no doubts other parts I've forgotten about. It's the last named which probably needs a few words of explanation. These fives courts were simply concreted outdoor areas, framed rather in the style of squash courts, where the antiquated game of fives was occasionally played. It involved opponents hitting a small ball off the walls whilst using either a bat or the gloved hands. I do recall that it wasn't a particularly popular past-time and was probably a legacy that lingered from the school's posh pre-war *Red Cap days. Away from the main school building there was also a School House, comprising various classrooms where some lessons also took place: I remember a music-room in particular, and also recall Sixth Formers would also occupy their own study upstairs.

Footnote: In the author's life time the school colours have remained predominantly purple with some orange, black and white stripes included, whereas in pre-war days the uniform was characterised by the wearing of a distinctive red cap, hence the nickname.

As for those cycle sheds, well the author's first school essay had the distinct misfortune to include as its opening sentence, *"The first thing that struck me when entering the school were the cycle sheds".* These innocuous words were immediately misconstrued and picked upon by a sadistic teacher and, as a result, the class hooted at it (and me) for weeks. But Tony has his own much more embarrassing memories of those times and it concerned his unusual surname. He recalls, *"I had a problem with the name McGinnity at school and some masters would jeeringly insist on pronouncing it with a soft G as in 'gin', the alcoholic spirit".* One can imagine the repetitive hurt, this insensitivity would cause. A more general embarrassment was to find oneself in a blazer, a tie and school cap with the majority of us also sporting short trousers for the first couple of years - oh, the shame of it all!

But all that would pass, and he did go on a couple of school trips, the first one of which comprised several days stay in the Lake District while part way through senior school, he became one of 28 pupils to visit Konigswinter in Germany. It was the first post-war trip undertaken by the school to Germany, and one wonders what subliminal influences he would absorb during this eventful 10 day visit? The school magazine report talks of them visiting the birthplace of Beethoven and then later taking in the Gothic splendour of Cologne Cathedral. One has to wonder how deep an impact all of these experiences must have had on the youthful Tony. Now back to those questions…

Question: *You were in The Mikado and the Yeoman of the Guard at senior school and I have the programmes to prove it. But were you in the later ones (Iolanthe/The Gondoliers) or had your voice broken by then?*

Answer: "Peep Bo" in the "Mikado" production. "Elsie Maynard" in "The Yeoman of the Guard" . Possibly chorus "Iolanthe", too. (Dressing up in drag was not my thing when puberty arrived!)

Comment: *The author has the programme for the 1952 school production of The Yeoman of the Guard with Tony listed as Elsie Maynard, a Strolling Singer. Likewise the 1953 programme for The Gondoliers where Tony (and the author) are listed as members of the chorus. But to illustrate how precocious Tony was he played a leading role in the December 1951 production of The Mikado although he had only arrived at the school a few months previous. His talent had been spotted.*

The school magazine gave him a mention, reporting the Mikado production thus: "it included McGinnity as Peep Bo, one of the Three Little Maids, and their voices blended well to form an interesting little trio." The following year (The Yeoman of the Guard) had the same condescending reviewer stating "McGinnity tackled the difficult part of Elsie Maynard with surprising success". Later productions saw him relegated to the chorus in The Gondoliers and Iolanthe, probably as a result of his voice having broken around that time.

I mentioned earlier that he was to lead the school orchestra too, whilst another musical string, already touched upon, found him performing as a soprano (often as a principal) in the Madrigal Society: giving recitals and concerts both within the school premises and sometimes further afield. It must have been draining but such was Tony's early musical prowess that more than one classmate remembers him having the energy left over to help him with his homework!

Question: *What was the misdemeanour at our school that led to you being carpeted? I believe the police were involved and this, I suspect, must have been circa 1955 or '56.*

Answer: It was a clarinet in the music room at school that caught my eye. As far as I could see nobody ever seemed to play it so one day I decided to take it. I was sure no one would notice its absence and I took it to a pawn shop in Norwich where, as a result, I got my first old battered guitar. The next day I was hauled into the headmaster's study (after the police had been in touch with the school) and I had a lot of explaining to do! Look, I was being trained in classical music. Nothing else was allowed - it was very restrictive.

Comment: *As can be seen, by the time the last year came around at school he was more than ready to move on and, in fact, he never really saw that last school year through. The extenuating circumstances for the rash action above (let's be kind and call it minor pilfering) were that he still didn't have a decent guitar and was desperate to get in front of an audience and express himself. He was also becoming a bit way-out in his demeanour and my pal Frank Hook recalls it this way: "I remember that when cutaway collars began to come in McGinnity arrived at school one day with his shirt collar adapted in that way, but having used his parents scissors to create the effect!" One hesitates to think of the subsequent ructions that this type of action caused his mother, his stepfather Jimmy, and any teacher he came into contact with!*

Now sometimes on a Monday, I've been known to stay in bed
There was something that I don't recall, and it done left my head
It can't be that important, 'cause I know I would remember
What went on last night and how come I got home this morning"

Four Day Workin' Week. Composer - Tony Sheridan

...one of the things that may have unsettled Tony, whose home life was always pretty fraught anyway, was when the family decided to move house, circa 1953, when he was exactly midway through his CNS schooling. One minute he was living in York Street, with the school almost on his doorstep, the next moment he was right out in the sticks, in the village of Thorpe St Andrew to be precise and faced with a lengthy daily commute to school. A hamlet a few miles east of Norwich, and situated well outside the City ring road it's often termed Thorpe Village, and guide books of the day would even describe it as the Richmond of Norfolk, which smacks somewhat of hyperbole. But, it's an ill-wind it's often said, and it wouldn't be very long before certain extra-curricula activities had taken over and he'd join a neighbourhood youth club with the aforesaid hip sounding name of the Thorpe St Andrew Teenage Club. Not only that but the stirrings of a new music were beginning to manifest themselves in most corners of post-war Britain.

Changes were in the air…

CHAPTER 3: The YOUTH CLUB YEARS - THE SAINTS ARE BORN

"You know my daddy was old
He never thought much of that rock 'n' roll
He thought I'd drive my mother round the bend"

When I was Young. Composer - Tony Sheridan

BACK-STORY: It was during 1955 that The Thorpe St Andrew Teenage Club first opened its doors and Tony wasn't the first member by any means. A hundred and three had enrolled before he walked through its doors, and chalked up number 104. It was a stroke of luck that the author managed to track down the former Thorpe Teenage Club secretary/treasurer, David Howard, and it was found, amazingly, that he was still diligently guarding the original exercise book wherein were listed the names and dates of birth of each and every youth club member who had passed through the club. And, more importantly for a conscientious treasurer, a note as to whether or not their annual subs had been paid for the year! David was also able to produce a small file of fading cuttings which he has lovingly preserved and these also helped to provide us with a few more clues as to what went on. The author also learnt the interesting fact that Tony had initially tried to join the rival Thorpe St Andrew youth club but, it's said, had become disruptive, and ended up getting ejected. It was this that led him to eventually join the bigger and definitely more hip-sounding Thorpe Teenage Club.

As can be imagined similar youth clubs to the above were springing up all over the country back then, remember the Teenager as a genre had just been invented, and such clubs had all sorts of activities designed to appeal to youngsters, ranging from table-tennis to chess indoors to the occasional forays outside whenever the weather permitted. There had always been the Scouts or the Boys' Brigade but youth clubs were more informal and let the members help pick the agenda. But perhaps the greatest appeal of such new clubs was the glorious opportunity to meet the opposite sex, and legitimately too! Coming from a boys-only Grammar school like the CNS this was one heck of a lure to a fast-maturing youth such as Tony. Then there was music: and it wouldn't be too long before a clique of lads, which included Tony as one of the ring-leaders, would get together with the idea of pounding out some of that new-fangled music that was beginning to be heard. Not classical music of course, but rock 'n' roll, and its British offshoot Skiffle, that was beginning to make itself heard louder by the day. The Saints (Tony's group) were about to be born and this was how they'd eventually line up: Tony McGinnity, vocals, guitar/violin, Andy Kinley on drums, John Taylor on T-chest bass/washboard, and Kenny Packwood lead guitar. Later they would add Mireille Gray (mainly to sing "Freight Train"!) and one or two other members that came and went, and they'll get a name-check later. But now, back to those questions…

Question: *Your group at Youth Club was called The Saints - how did that name originate, or is it obvious? (Firstly, the group were formed in Thorpe St Andrew, and then, secondly there was the popular number "When the Saints Go Marching In", which most amateur groups would include in their repertoire. Where else could it come from?")*

Answer: As a 16 year old skiffler the name The Saints came to me as a revelation, a piece of pure genius. Sadly, as I later discovered, there were at least two other *groups - albeit in other parts of the country - sporting the same genial name.

* *Footnote*: Author - I recall Tony mentioning that on getting to London, circa 1958, he discovered that both Stevie Winwood and Russ Sainty had been involved with outfits that included Saints as part of their titles: so he was more than happy to jettison the name from the outset.

Comment: *I think he's surely being facetious in saying the name came to him as a revelation. He would later explain that the name was inspired by the Saint character from the pen of author Leslie Charteris. This certainly rings more true as the author spotted (from an old photo of the group) the Saint halo painted on the side of their tea-chest bass. It's also worth pointing out that The Saints was a creation that only existed in Tony's Norwich days and the name was abandoned the moment he left for the lights of London, as was the name McGinnity. That episode comes up in a following chapter. We've briefly mentioned the main group members names but to do them justice, and rather than disrupt the story further, a detailed run-down of the group is included in a separate appendix. And there's more on that very glamorous young female member!*

Question: *You played at Thorpe Red Lion - were you The Saints at that time?*

Answer: The Art School pub was definitely a "Red Lion". The Thorpe pub may have been a "White Lion" or similar. 1956 saw the birth of the "Saints". We won £15 at the Industrial Club in Norwich, against assorted all-comers. On occasion we also played at the "Cottage" pub in Thorpe St. Andrew.

Comment: *Of all the many venues that the Saints played back then the main one tended to be that Red Lion pub opposite the Art School, and a few years ago the local Norwich paper tracked down the local pub landlady who remembered those times: "when Tony Sheridan played our pub it was packed. The people would stand outside on the pavement trying to hear him. He was only a lad". So it was depressing for the author to discover the premises all boarded up and, although it has now reopened as a bar, it bears no resemblance to the venue where Tony performed back then. But fortunately not so the Art School itself which still thrives and was the place where TS was to put in that single term or so of so-called work before the music drug proved too strong, and he finally dropped out of formal schooling for good. But we need to hear more about that skiffle competition, which we'll describe next, under a rather fanciful title of Local Skiffle Kings. The author is grateful to a local source for what appears next:*

Local Skiffle Kings

Tony's brief mention that the group won £15 is almost dismissive in tone but it was quite a big deal back then and even made the local Norwich papers: as did the news that The Saints were also used to promote the showing of the latest Tommy Steele film which had just reached Norwich. The group (well, Tony really) was beginning to become big fish in a very small pond and it wouldn't be long before he would be dreaming of horizons far beyond Norfolk. On a separate front, although success appeared to be coming their way they remained as poor as church mice and usually (it's rather embarrassing to recall) had to transport their own instruments by bus, or bike, to whatever venue they were playing next. Then, at the height of the skiffle craze in Norwich (June 1957 to be precise) the group, along with a handful or other contestants, would find themselves competing for the title of the area's best skiffle group and it's probably no surprise to learn that Tony and his pals ran off with the title and the money, although memories differ as to the exact amount. Mind you, they had the intense satisfaction of vanquishing several other local groups, in particular The Cygnets and The Vampires, who we're told finished as joint runners-up.

Among other events, the group also found themselves playing as part of a Grand Variety Show that was put on by the club members at a Thorpe school in May of 1957 with the Saints shown as doing a set before the interval, as were an accordionist and two other club members who did a spot of mime! Perhaps fortunately, no-one can remember too much detail about this actual gig but again it did get a write-up in the local newspaper by way of posterity. A much bigger event occurred around the same time and involved that local screening of The Tommy Steele Story: The Saints were readily available (and no doubt cheaper to hire) than Tommy Steele and the Steelmen. Occasional group member John Taylor recalls that the film was being shown for a week and the group found themselves thrust into the spotlight on the opening night when they had the daunting job of providing some interval action for the theatre's captive audience. It was quite an innovative idea at the time, certainly for Britain, and so while the audience ate or queued for ice-creams, Tony and his pals energetically went through their repertoire of skiffle numbers on stage. In reality this meant performing as many popular numbers of the day ("Heartbreak Hotel" was one favourite) as the allotted interval slot would allow them to cram in. What's certain is that they certainly played in front of the biggest audience of their short careers to date. John Taylor also remembers that earlier that day, prior to the screening, the group had played on the back of a lorry of sorts which trundled around the City streets while advertising the film. Back to more questions…

Question: *For Tony the name of Lonnie Donegan looms large in his influences, probably above all others, so I asked him which recording had first inspired him. The answer was obvious.*

Answer: From 1956, when I first heard Lonnie Donegan's recording of 'Rock Island Line' I was hooked on becoming a professional musician. Hearing American-style music when quite young, sort of conditioned the mind to receive what was to ensue after the 'Blackboard Jungle' film (1955) catapulted Bill Haley and the hit 'Rock Around the Clock' into prominence. When Gene Vincent and Elvis Presley appeared - well, there was no looking back. Of course, for a while I was at Art School, pretending to study fine art. But I never wanted to do anything else - professionally speaking - other than perform, write, record, all that. It was in my blood, just waiting to emerge.

Comment: *Donegan really just exploded on the British scene with "Rock Island Line". And, it's well-known, he was no wallflower and had his own brash way of describing himself right from the start: "I am Skiffle!" he would modestly say. While later, another part-humorous, part-sacrilegious, quote of Lonnie's was "in the beginning was the Word, and the Word was made Lon!" And I'm sure there's plenty more where that came from. But for now Tony's scene remained confined to the immediate locality, revolving around the Art School scene and within the City itself or the occasional gig in*

Thorpe. To briefly inject a personal memory here, I remember being a member of a youth club in another neighbourhood and so didn't see so much of Tony at this point. But I do vividly recall seeing at least one of their gigs, at The Blue Room on the Prince of Wales Road in the centre of Norwich, which was probably just prior to their first London foray. And I remember they were good, very good.

While all of this talk of skiffle and The Saints was going on we mustn't forget that TS would also name the first song they ever performed in public was at an unknown village hall and was their version of another Donegan hit "Don't You Rock Me Daddy-O". Sometime during the lifetime of the group they also decided to record four songs on a domestic tape machine, although it seems certain that the cassette tape in question has long since disappeared. Tony himself has no recollection of such a tape although Saints member John Taylor clearly recalls some sort of cassette being made in the Assembly Hall of the St William's Way School in Thorpe and thinks that in addition to their debut song, the other songs included the perennial "Worried Man Blues" that The Vipers or Donegan would often perform back then, and also "Midnight Special". Back to more questions...

Question: *It seems that Tony didn't have too much to say about The Saints era although in recalling those early amateur days with fondness, he would admit -*

Answer: We had a good group, *and he would point out*, we had real drums.

Comment: *Not as flippant as it might seem. Most amateur skiffle groups would content themselves with just the trademark washboard: impressively The Saints had both!*

Question: *At this point we must let Tony sum up in his own words, just why he was so desperate to leave the confines of Norwich. Here's how he put it and, if the decision was difficult for everyone else, it presumably wasn't for him.*

Answer: It seemed at the time that everyone was against our music. Being a skiffle or rock 'n' roll man in the Norwich of the late Fifties was akin to being one of the Kray twins *(author's note: famous gangster figures of the day).* I had to leave - I had to get my freedom. I thought Norwich was destined to be termed a Fine Conservative City for ever. Skiffle had turned me on so I got rid of my pimples, got my guitar and headed off down the A 11 road to the bright lights.

Comment: *To explain that reference. The road signs that welcome you as you entered Norwich then, as now, proclaim the legend: Norwich - *A Fine City. And it may have seemed politically Conservative too, although it wouldn't always remain that way. He would certainly have lost his pimples when he set off down the notorious A11 Norwich/London road in the naïve hope that they might achieve instant fame, given the journey was not easy back then. And, by the way, notorious is still the word for the A-11 as even today (2013) it remains a single-carriageway in places, having originally been tabled to be up-graded under Edward Heath's government back in 1971! (It is now scheduled to be completed by Winter, 2014).*

**Footnote:* The description of Norwich as "a fine City" goes back to the 19th century having been originally coined by the well-known Norwich author George Borrow (1803-1881).

...but before we turn to the London scene that awaited TS we must first add another snippet about the Teenage Club before it disappears for ever from our pages. As mentioned, it had first opened its doors to Thorpe's teenagers from late 1955, the Secretary labelling that first year's intake as Year 1955/56. The club would continue running through the '50s before the records finally petered out at the end of the fourth year (1958/9), curiously a period that almost symbolises the demise of rock 'n' roll itself. During those four years some 245 members would pass through the club's doors including all of the Saints members mentioned earlier, with the exception of Ms Gray and Alan Callf, who were not in the group from the start and were occasional members only.

The first of these was a particularly attractive young lady with the striking, if unusual name, of Mireille Gray . She would briefly be to The Saints what Nancy Whiskey was to Chas McDevitt, soloing at gigs on the group's own well-remembered version of "Freight Train" but, when asked by the author what else she sang, she couldn't particularly recall any other numbers! But, hey, that's okay. Crucially a couple of years younger than the others (she was born in 1942) there would have been no way her parents would sanction anything as outrageous as an un-chaperoned trip to the Nation's capital so sadly she was left behind when the first London expedition finally took place. (Or was she? As another member of the Youth Club insists she did go to London and had to be fetched back!) The other occasional member was a local amateur musician and guitarist Alan Callf who, having been born back in January of 1937, was quite a bit older than the others and was part way through an engineering apprenticeship. Handily he lived just around the corner from Tony in Thorpe so now and again he would find himself standing in with The Saints, especially after Kenny Packwood stayed on in London and Tony temporarily returned to Norwich.

By now Tony had created a bit of a name for himself but it was all contained within the county border and almost within the boundary of Norwich itself. But 1957 had arrived (the Saints would play their final gig on 18th November that year) and a most pivotal year it would turn out to be for him and every other aspiring British musician. It was to be Skiffle music's one soaring year although to get anywhere Tony still knew deep-down that he needed to exchange the pub lights of Norwich for the brighter ones of London even if, in the process, it meant that he might end up leaving his old chums behind. But for the time being most of them were still with him and some were about to head into the distance by literally thumbing their way along the then single-carriageway A-11 road that meandered southwards down towards London. Although a quartet of them were to make that first trip only Tony, and Kenny for a time, would really stay the course long term and, in Tony's case, make the permanent decision to turn his back on his birthplace...

CHAPTER 4: AN UNLIKELY NEXT STOP - The SEA SCOUTS!

"When we were young
We were groovin' fast
Everyone said rock 'n' roll won't last
Sure was a stupid thing to say"

When I Was Young - composer Tony Sheridan

BACK-STORY: At the end of the last chapter we had Tony about to leave for London but before we get there we really need to cover another hidden fragment of his teenage years. No, not the Art School which has been briefly touched upon, but rather an abortive attempt to emulate our local county and national hero, Lord Nelson ("I am a Norfolk man and glory in being so") by embarking upon a life on the briny. Tony had already junked his school uniform and embraced the informality of the arts college where the surroundings were far more laid back and relaxed, as befitted such a bohemian subject. Unsurprisingly Tony had always been desperate to avoid the convention of an office job and so a compromise of sorts was reached with his parents whereby he supposedly continued to expand his mind, if not his finances, by briefly attempting the study of fine art.

But better than this, the change of scenery also had the effect of expanding his circle of musical contacts. Life was at last beginning to look up, even if home-life continued to be stressful for all concerned. It may be a digression but his mother was forever trying to help steer his life in some new direction or another - one that would help use up his boundless energy and point him in the right direction, whatever that was. She'd even sanctioned him joining the local boxing club (The Lads Club in King Street) but that was short-lived. Soon she suggested that the teenage Anthony ought to consider joining the local Sea Scouts: it sounds unlikely but it's an intriguing story even if it turned out to be nothing more than a dead end. But it's definitely worth recounting in some detail before we move on to the lights of London. The following paraphrases Tony's words, as does the section which follows immediately after.

(1) A Life on the Ocean Waves - well...almost

It may only be a blip in our story but this is briefly when his life almost changed direction for ever, and it was sometime around his 16th birthday. He'd had a stab at being a land-based Boy Scout but now the idea grew that he might be able to continue scouting while simultaneously being afloat! Luckily, there was a thriving Sea Scout pack on the outskirts of Norwich, not far from his home, and it was this new venture that was to have unexpected repercussions and might even have led him towards a naval career if fate hadn't intervened on behalf of the young McGinnity. So what happened? Well, Tony recalls that his time with the Sea Scouts opened up the distinct possibility of gaining a place at the highly esteemed Dartmouth Naval College and, with his mother's approval and with this goal now firmly in his sight, he'd apprehensively made his way to London, kitted up as smartly as a nervous young man could, to end up facing a frightening panel of inquisitors.

The interview in question took place aboard the HMS Chrysanthemum (sic?) and he assumed that the intimidating line-up he was facing were all retired admirals or similar luminaries. All he can remember for sure thereafter is that the meeting didn't seem to be going too well until, as a last resort, he decided to launch into an impassioned, heartfelt plea during which he gave full vent to his innermost, suppressed feelings. Miraculously, he feels this tactic must have swayed the panel and turned an impending disaster into a success, as he was told that he'd passed the interview and presumably was on his way to a life on the ocean waves. But that joy would soon turn sour when he had to visit a naval hospital and undergo what seemed to him the relative formality of a medical examination. It was then that he realised that, although his general fitness rivalled that of any other 16 year old, the problem was his apparent colour-blindness. Clearly he was and remains colour-blind but it was just something he'd accepted as normal and had never really thought much about: certainly not as something to be any sort of bar to his progress in life. But it clearly was, and that was all there was to it. (In fact, even to this day he cannot distinguish between the changing colours of traffic lights, although it's a handicap he's had to live with and as a result he has never driven a car.)

The immediate and practical outcome to the above was a disappointing return to Norwich to look at his remaining options, given that the prospect of a naval career was denied him. And so we return again to Tony's continuing exertions as a skiffle-playing Saint where, although increasingly successful, for the moment any fame would remain localised and confined to in and around Norwich. But he was surely only biding his time and it wouldn't be too long before the first of several London excursions would come about, fame was without doubt awaiting him and maybe his pals too, if they had the courage to join him.

(2) The Journey to the 2 I's Coffee Bar

Of the half-dozen occasional members of The Saints it was to be Kenny, Andy and Dougie who TS persuaded to accompany him to London on that first exploratory excursion. John Taylor would recall some details of that time in a letter to the author, "Dougie, as far as I can remember was more of a fan of the group and used to follow us around on gigs. To the best of my knowledge he didn't play any "pukka" musical instrument, but dabbled with the T-chest bass and when I decided not to go to London on the first trip, he took my place in the group. The group members on that trip were Tony, Kenny, Andy, Doug and Mireille Gray. I recall that Andy, Doug and Mireille came home rather quickly, especially Mireille whose parents shot up to London to retrieve her! I'm not sure how the group got to London, but I believe they travelled in a borrowed van, driver unknown". That's probably as detailed a description of that first expedition as we'll get despite the fact that John wasn't actually present - but it was all a very long time ago.

Dougie, who certainly was there, can still vividly remember trying out at the *2 I's Coffee Bar and encountering a host of other itinerant musicians, one of whom was more flamboyant than most of the others put together. This was the rock 'n' roll wanabee Wee Willie Harris who, with his prototype-punk coloured hair and outlandish suits, was a real shock to the system for the audiences (and of course the musicians) that encountered him in London in those early days. Incidentally Wee Willie Harris, whose name was really Charles William Harris, had the misfortune to find that his best chance of success, a record called "Rockin' at the 2 I's", would fail to get BBC radio play on the grounds that it was indirectly endorsing the 2 I's establishment, and therefore had a commercial angle that was deemed unacceptable. That was the way things were back then: but Willie has had the last laugh and has never stopped working to this day.

**Footnote*: There's more on this legendary Old Compton Street venue in a Glossary entry. The former site where all those musical hopefuls trekked to is now honoured by it's own Green Plaque, even if the premises itself is now largely unrecognisable.

Having been knocked back on his first fleeting visit to London, TS would soon make a second assault on the capital - this time it really had nothing to do with The Saints but it purely involved the ever-hyper Tony, accompanied by his neighbourhood friend, fellow guitarist and standby Saint - and (more luckily!) motor bike owner Alan Callf. Now, whether or not it was solely Alan's musical prowess or the more pertinent fact that he just happened to own a means of transportation is a question perhaps best left hanging in the air. What can be stated for sure is that Alan was also totally besotted at this point by the musical sounds of the day, and in direct contrast, even more disenchanted with his engineering day job.

And so it came about that, climbing aboard as pillion on 21 year old Alan's 199cc 1954 model Triumph Tiger Cub bike one snowy Winter's day, the yet-to-turn 18 year old TS and his pal Alan Callf embarked on what would turn out to be a pretty hair-raising journey to London, or as it was colloquially known to one and all The Smoke. Tony somehow managed to cling on to his friend's back but it couldn't have been too easy: a trip made all the more perilous by deep snow almost from the moment that they exchanged the outskirts of Norwich for the wilds of Norfolk and beyond. As can be imagined both men took minimal luggage with them and there was hardly room for a guitar to be slung between them. And that throws up a subject of some sensitivity between the respective (or should that be selective?) memories of Tony and Alan, for the latter is sure that he can't ever remember seeing TS with a guitar of his own! His recollection is of Tony managing to beg or borrow someone else's guitar in those early days so desperate was he to perform. Remember the earlier story of the purloined clarinet?

To completely unravel the next year or so as it relates to our main man, has not been easy although we know for certain that there were at least two trips to London after that first foray with The Saints that was mentioned earlier. And it's also certain that the second attempt was during the snowy wiles of that January and that it was just the two of them that would fit aboard the bike. Asked recently about that 100+ mile bike trip, Tony the precarious pillion passenger, could only say with some emotion, *"it did my kidneys in for life!"* (Sadly, and with an ironic twist, Tony would give that quote to the author a full year <u>before</u> he needed to have a kidney removed to save his life! Oh dear, what a terrible irony.) Thereafter, despite leaving their mate and ace guitarist Kenny in London, the remaining Saints had little option but to re-group and revive their local name back in Norfolk, permanently drafting in guitarist Alan Callf to bolster their line-up.

Alan confessed to the author that he'd realised from the first moment of his arrival in London that the life of an itinerant musician was not one that he relished, although he has happily had a lifelong involvement with the local music scene playing as an amateur with such local groups as The Toffs and The Zodiacs, but all the while holding down that engineering job until retirement finally beckoned a few years ago. And for Alan there had at least been the fleeting thrill of being on the fringe of things and getting to meet other pop hopefuls of the day such as *Vince Eager, and Tommy Steele's brother, *Colin Hicks and a handful of others who were in the process of signing up to become members of *Larry Parnes' pop stable. Not only that but (presumably because of Tony's girl appeal) Alan also recalls them staying at the debutante Annarella Flower's London flat for a few days. Eye-opening stuff maybe but not a way of life that held out any appeal to the new boy from 'the sticks'.

Footnote: For more details regarding all of those indicated with an asterisk above please see the relevant Glossary entries. Colin Hicks is mentioned in the entry relating to that of his brother, Tommy Steele.

Meanwhile that second return trip to Norwich was, in effect, only to draw up a plan of campaign that would ultimately see Tony severing his links with his home city for good and all. While he perversely doesn't really think of himself as an exile nevertheless to this day he rarely returns, such visits having become even more spasmodic as the years have rolled by. As to the renewed assault on London his biker friend Alan, like the other members of The Saints before him, was as mentioned to last just the one week before deciding that the bright lights were not for him and he would return home to set about completing the engineering apprenticeship and a life of stability that he'd come precariously close to giving up. Let's turn to Tony's answers about those London days, he's got plenty to say about that heady time, a time that would soon lead into the Swinging Sixties…

CHAPTER 5 : THE LATE '50s - LONDON AND THE 2 I's SCENE

"Let me tell you straight, back in '58
I made me some money on a beat-up guitar
Doin' the Ubangi Stomp with a wiggle and a bomp
At the gig in the Alligator bar"

Won't Do It Again. Composer - Tony Sheridan

BACK-STORY: It's 1958 and the British singles charts were almost solidly American rock 'n' roll with Elvis, Buddy Holly, The Everly Brothers and Jerry Lee Lewis and assorted others monopolising both our radio waves and, occasionally, our TV screens too, although a British fight back was beginning spearheaded by our very own Elvis in the shape of Cliff Richard. And a TV monopoly it certainly was back then as, with only two channels available, the scene was literally carved up between the stolid 'auntie' BBC and the commercial newcomer, ITV. As to the radio (or wireless as it was still mainly termed) there was even less competition with the State run BBC effectively having a monopoly. As can be guessed tracking down the pop records of the day wasn't that easy, which is perhaps why a generation of youngsters went about with a transistor set glued to their ears as they strove to keep a dodgy signal from Radio Luxembourg or AFN (American Forces Network) tuned in. It was to be during the '60s, that the real sea change in the accessibility of pop and rock music would come about, something we now take for granted. In contrast the youth back then had to listen out for request programmes such as the daily Housewife's Choice or Two Way Family Favourites at the weekend to hear something remotely pop. For a while it was a pretty dire scene on the surface, but incredibly exciting if you knew where to look. And it was getting better...

Question: *You were in what groups in the 50s/60s? Confirm The Worried Men, The Jets, The Big Six, The Star Combo and Vince Taylor and the Playboys for starters.*

Answer: Although we knew each other from the Soho scene, I was never a member of the "Worried Men". "The Jets" (from "West Side Story") was not my idea - in fact, I thought the name was slightly vulgar. The "Tony Sheridan Trio" was more to the point and less pretentious. (I thought the names "Troggs" and "Rocking Berries" went too far...).

After our first stint together in Hamburg, "The Beatles" remained just that - and most of my bands were - for recording purposes - known as "The Beat Brothers". (This name came into being because the record company thought that: "Tony Sheridan and the Beatles," sounded - to German ears - somehow offensive). Bobby Patrick's "Big Six" from Glasgow backed me 64-67 - a fine group. "Star Combo" was a synthetic group, formed solely to perform at the "Star Club" 1962-63, and featured, amongst others, Roy Young on piano and vocals.

Comment: *Tony has brought the Beatles up prematurely here - it will be their turn very soon. He hasn't mentioned it here but he told me that when in London, ever the rebel and non-conformist, he found himself auditioning for The City Ramblers, a somewhat purist skiffle group, who promptly set about pulling his style apart by awarding ticks and crosses against the musical elements that made up his overall playing style! Oh dear, it was all too restrictive and too much like school for him so, needless to* *say he wasn't bothered at all when that particular door failed to open. A basic list of the groups he appeared with, or fronted, from the late 1950s through to his departure to Vietnam are given in Appendix No. 3. It is worth adding here that The Beat Brothers of Hamburg are not to be confused with The Beat Boys, a Larry Parnes outfit from the late '50s, who backed Dickie Pride and Johnny Gentle among others: curiously, Kenny Packwood, who went down to London with Tony Sheridan was at one time a member of The Beat Boys and later, when he went to Germany, The Beat Brothers.*

Question: *Did you deal with the impresario Don Arden at all? If so I'll have some supplementary questions. (I was aware TS had first met up with Don Arden, a budding impresario at this point, when he first travelled to London.)*

Answer: All us budding young musicians had to do with the likes of Don Arden. There were three main "impresarios" - Larry Parnes, Tito Burns, and Don Arden. Don was, in many ways, the most sympathetic of the three. There was something of the genus of the market place vendor about him, a loud and blustery extrovert and an instinctive understanding of artistes - or of boxers or wrestlers! Don, Paul Lincoln (Dr. Death), Ray Hunter and Les Bristow were all at least in my opinion - of a similar kind. I liked him. When he asked : "Howzit going Tony?" he meant it. I worked for him on several tours. Later he came over to Hamburg to book some of his acts at the "Star Club", etc.

Comment: *As is fairly well known the late Don Arden is Sharon Osbourne's father (Sharon being the wife of Ozzy Osbourne) and father and daughter were estranged for years before being reconciled a few years before his death. It's reported that in his day Don Arden's style of pop management was pretty uncompromising and Tony is probably one of the few to reminisce fondly about him. (see Glossary entry, Don Arden, for further details.)*

Question: *Out of curiosity did you ever meet Joe Meek? (To fans of a certain figure Joe Meek - see Glossary - is a legendary record producer who Tony might just have visited in those early days.)*

Answer: Never met Joe Meek, fate probably knew several good reasons why I should not meet certain persons from the "business"...

Comment: *This checks out of course. In John Repsch's definitive biography of Meek Tony's name isn't mentioned.*

Question: *Was there any possibility of being in the UK stable of Larry Parnes with the others?*

Answer: We were all aware that Parnes was "gay" (in today's language) and partial to young singers and musicians. He made a "pass" at me - to no avail. I detested the guy then - now I might feel sorry for him. We musicians often debated whether the singers in his stable were involved with him personally... (Probably not - at least, not the more famous of them). Parnes did not see me as a "commercial commodity" anyway. On the other hand, he hired me primarily as a backing musician, and I was "allowed" to sing a couple of numbers, too!

Brian Liquorice Locking (bass) came down to Soho from Lincoln with Roy Taylor (aka Vince Eager). We joined forces with Brian Bennett on drums to back Vince Eager and Vince Taylor, amongst others. We also played the West End nightclubs, e.g. "Winstons" or "Churchills". (Quite recently, *Big Jim Sullivan told me that he rated me as "probably the best rock guitarist in the U.K." back in the late fifties. That was new to me!) *Later TS would explain to the author:* Look I was happy not to be contracted to Larry Parnes. But we had an open arrangement and I could and was offered things. Remember, not many others were playing good guitar back then so I had something to offer him. It was a mutual thing.

**Footnote*: Sadly Big Jim Sullivan (1941-2012) would pass away whilst this book was in course of preparation.

Comment: *It's worth adding that Larry Parnes (Mr Parnes, Shillings and Pence) who as a pop mogul would live in a swish house in Knightsbridge had recently signed up Tony's Norwich pal Kenny Packwood as a guitar player (he would become one of Marty Wilde's Wildcats for a while) and had insisted that he would line up some gigs for Tony in the near future if he'd return to London. As Tony recounts it, "I had to go back to Norwich for a time but I literally counted the days till I would return and knock on his door and make him keep his promise. I also knew from the minute I arrived at the 2 I's that I would have to have an electric guitar." There's a bit more on Larry Parnes in the Glossary. And whilst we're talking guitarists there's a Jimmy Page quote saying, "the only guitarist at that time who was any good was Tony Sheridan."*

Question: *What about Henry Henroid? (Gene Vincent's manager back then). Sounds a bit of a nutter (allegedly) - any anecdotes? (Methinks I should have contrived to antagonize Tony more often as this question led to an extremely detailed and hugely interesting reply).*

Answer: I loved the guy. (Resent the "nutter" remark). Henry was a warm, good-natured Cockney who, along with others, formed a solid "buffer" fraternity of well-wishers in Soho 1957-60. Soho was, in effect, an island, vaguely resembling Greenwich Village in its aims and trends, especially in the music field (Alexis Korner, Chas McDevitt, Ronny Scott etc. etc.) Henry was part of a team comprising Paul Lincoln, Ray Hunter, Tom Littlewood ("2 I's"). Everything happened in Old Compton Street, Wardour Street and there were about 40 regular personalities who meant something, of whom Henry was one of a - generally speaking - enigmatic lot. Shame nobody came up with the idea of filming a few typical 1957-59 Soho days/weeks…

As Bob Dylan says about the decline of the creative 'alive' Greenwich Village period, Soho met with a similar fate towards the end of the fifties. Just another example of how transient and sensitive a live artistic movement is when - as in our case - it originates <u>from</u> the people, <u>for</u> the people. And then someone ruins it all by selling out to big business, and the media really messes things up. (At this point, just a thought: what a tremendous chance for humanity to grow and mature was lost in the German Democratic Republic. There the emergence of an awful autocratic system, in which egocentric idiots were able to make a career by the use of angst and total control.)

Some of the personalities comprising the Soho crowd of 1957-60:
Paul Lincoln, Ray Hunter, Wee Willie Harris, Terry Nelhams (Adam Faith), Joe Brown, Cliff Richard, Hank Marvin, Bruce Welch, Roy Taylor (Vince Eager), Vince Taylor, Brian Bennett, Brian "Liquorice" Locking, Worried Men, Vipers/Wally Whyton, Les

Bennets, Zom, Chas Beaumont, Big Roy, "2 I's" Norman, Les Bristow and Nora, Chas McDevitt, Roger "the Dodger", Roy Young, Terry Dene, Lionel Bart, Tex Makin, Joe Singer, Don Arden, Red Reece, Jet Harris, Chris Andrews, Bobby Woodman, Russ Sainty, Ronny Scott, Freddy Lloyd, Annarella Flower and Caroline, Mickie Most and Alex ("The Most Brothers") and others.

Comment: *Tony must have been in a hugely reflective mood when he dredged his memory banks to come up with that fairly inclusive list of personalities from that era. He could have gone on to also mention the venues - apart from the 2 I's there was the Skiffle Cellar, the Cat's Whiskers and a rash of others. As to individuals he could sometimes be cutting: "There was no love lost between me and Vince Eager" was one such comment, to which he then added, "I liked rock 'n' roll to be authentic and not sung by a shaky-voiced guy from Grantham". A withering remark maybe, but he's surely entitled to his opinion even if it is pretty forthright. Many of the other names will be known to those of a certain age but Zom was one the author had not heard of. Seems to have been a fairly humorous and lugubrious individual who played in several skiffle groups including The Vipers and Chas McDevitt. Was at the outset not averse to busking in the street, if it was really necessary. (There are entries in the Glossary for Henry Henroid and a few others that Tony lists.)*

Lincoln and Hunter (also above) ran the 2 I's at one time but were also involved in the professional wrestling scene, the former using the intimidating name of Doctor Death! Russ Sainty had only minimal success as a solo artist but was later to join The Dallas Boys and stay in the business. If readers want to know more, such niche publications as The Restless Generation by Pete Frame or Hamburg The Cradle of British Rock by Alan Clayson need to be sought out. (See Bibliography).

Question: *You made nine appearances (some sources give a different figure) on TV in "Oh Boy!" - did Jack Good (in effect) axe you? Did this mean you were blacklisted from similar shows from those days, Boy Meets Girl, etc?*

Answer: Oh, Alan, nobody "axed" me! I just lost interest and "forgot" my guitar or made a general nuisance of myself. Felt used or under-rated, Think I told you once before that playing and performing is a great privilege. The "business" repulses me. Guess I'm a bit of a quirk - but I'm still alive and kickin', and my life has been a fantastic, amazing experience. You've obviously no idea how thankful I am for this gift of life as a free musician in an awfully messed-up world. My main obstacle has been that beauty (any kind!) fascinates me - music, art, nature, life; and I'm a sucker for a pretty face! Oh, Alan! Of course I was not "blacklisted or similar" from anything. (Where do you get this stuff from, godammit?)

Comment: *Occasionally Tony can get a bit selective where his memory is concerned. The good news is that his tardiness in not toeing the line in those early days probably led indirectly to him leaving these shores and finding success in Germany. As a postscript to those days Tony met up with Jack Good when the latter was in London producing an Elvis musical, "but he couldn't even remember me! But he did a lot in his time to legitimise the music".*

Question: *Did you get involved in any of the flurry of shows from the '60s, such* *as Thank You Lucky Stars, etc?*

Answer: In June '60 I moved to Hamburg, disgusted (as many of us were) with the British "scene" and recording industry. (All we heard was: "rock 'n' roll is nearly out, guitar bands, too, etc. etc"). Nevertheless I did do the occasional TV show (or whatever - e.g. Pathe Pictorial '64/'65, filmed in Stratford-on-Avon). I took what came, as it were. If something presented itself, I usually did it...Lots of TV in Germany - to this day.

Comment: *It's been written elsewhere that having been dropped from the "Oh Boy!" show - one version has him missing rehearsals - he then lost the chance to join the cast of the Boy Meets Girl TV series which was to follow shortly.*

Question: *Read somewhere you were in Lord Rockingham's X1?*

Answer: I was never a member of "Lord R's X1". Maybe they accompanied me a couple of times on TV's "Oh Boy!" show. My mate, Kenny Packwood, guitar player did join Lord R's. (Kenny and I were both in the "Saints" in Norwich. He went to the CNS school, too - a year behind us!). He was already an accomplished jazz musician. We joined up again in 1960/1 in Hamburg. Later he joined the Royal Marines as a musician.

Comment: *Of course, Lord Rockingham's X1 are still fondly remembered for their U.K. 1958 No.1 "Hoots Mon", which would chart again in 1993. Frustratingly, the whereabouts of Kenny Packwood still remains unknown.*

Question: *You were on Cherry Wainer's 1959 record 'cover' of the US hit "The Happy Organ" by Dave "Baby" Cortez. Were you on any other recordings during that period - e.g. The Worried Men? (see Glossary entry under Wainer's name for more on this).*

Answer: Vince Taylor's "Right Behind You Baby", with Brian Bennett and Liquorice Locking. Also Brenda Lee's "What'd I Say" produced by Mickie Most. But not The Worried Men.

Comment: *The author had heard it rumoured that Tony may have briefly been with the latter group during the '50s: he wasn't.*

Question: *What about your contemporary from the Soho scene, Joe Brown?*

Answer: *Joe and I used to vie for our audience' favour in the 2 I's. We both did alright - although I never did quite grasp how it was that he could sing with a Cockney accent and get away with it. (Even Tommy Steele had to knuckle under, mixing in Memphis mutterings to balance out the Bermondsey bel canto). Joe gained my personal respect for his proficiency on the electric guitar - in those days a rarity. He said a few nice things about my playing, too. As I recall, we both thought *Hank (Marvin) sold himself out by: (a) playing with Cliff. (b) by performing silly instrumental music like "Apache", etc.

**Footnote:* As Tony was on the Cochran/Vincent tour with Joe Brown there's an entry in the Glossary under Joe's name. Hank Marvin (born Brian Rankin in 1941) needs little description here, being the distinctive lead guitarist with the Shadows over many decades as well as being identified with Cliff Richard. Cliff needs even less of an introduction and can still be found performing on stage, or in a recording studio and even occasionally helping out at Wimbledon if called upon. In other words he's a British institution.

Comment: *Strong words - I hope no Shadows fans are reading! And for the uninitiated bel canto literally means "a style of operatic singing in a pure and even tone".*

Question: *Anything to say re *P. J. Proby? We (i.e. rock 'n' roll fans) often wondered at one time whether he was 'genuine' years ago as he claimed to make demos for Elvis as Marcus Smith.*

**Footnote:* Born James Marcus Smith in Texas in 1938, Proby seems to have spent most of his career based in the UK where he has occasionally made the news - and sometimes for the wrong reasons. A colourful character who has never fully escaped his trouser-splitting days of the '60s - not even in this brief entry nearly 50 years later! But he has gone on to appear in the West End in stage musicals, most famously in the role of Elvis in a production put together by pop producer Jack Good.

Answer: Sad. He did (as all US singers did) earn a bit (by sounding "like Elvis") when publishers/songwriters were trying to sell songs to establish artistes like Elvis.

Comment: *A seemingly gratuitous question but I dropped in the occasional pop 'name' thinking it might well prompt a reminiscence. But not so on this occasion!*

Question: *Any comments re your contemporary Eric Clapton?*

Answer: Oh, Eric Clapton! One day it became apparent to me that he is an ambassador, sent from above to assist in the healing process of our planet. God bless him and his music. (Personally, I find Santana's music more to my current taste - but it's close).

Comment: *Both Eric and Tony in their individual way are true troubadours of song, and both can play a bit of guitar too! Clapton really doesn't need a Glossary entry.*

Question: *Tony, approximately how many songs have you written? Do you consider yourself primarily a song-writer? Probably you hate being pigeon-holed. (The author had misspelled 'pigeon' as 'pidgeon' so an English class from a German resident follows).*

Answer: About 28 good songs - and approx 100 crappy ones. As I write this, I'm becoming a writer, too. Seriously, I'm really a song-writer on occasion.

And it's not "pidgeon-holed" - it's "pigeonholed" or "pidgin-holed". Hate them all, anyway.

Comment: *Good answer Tony. I recall Buddy Holly being interviewed by Dick Clark on American Bandstand circa 1958 and indicating that he (Holly) had written only 15 or so songs. Better surely quality, than quantity.*

Question: *Did you know that Gene Vincent played the Maddermarket Coffee Bar in 1971 in Norwich, the year he died? A reference book at that time said that an Earl Sheridan was hassling him for money. Tony, not implying this was you, but did you know an Earl S?*

Answer: No, but I hope to appear in Norwich myself before the bucket is kicked! Earl Sheridan? - no idea; perhaps you could track the SOB down?

Comment: *The author has since answered his own question. Earl Sheridan produced many of the final gigs that Gene did in the UK, circa 1971. Sadly, they were poorly supported and this resulted in wrangles between the singer and producer in dividing up the meagre receipts.*

Question: *Need to know who you toured with in the '60s , e.g. Cochran/Vincent tour as The Tony Sheridan Trio. Did you back Brenda Lee? Ditto Conway Twitty? On bills with who else, Roy Orbison?*

Answer No.1: Two tours with Conway Twitty (he especially asked for me through *Henry Henroid). Brenda Lee tour (but not backing her), Johnny Preston, Freddy Cannon, Chubby Checker, etc. *Vince Eager from the UK and Cliff Richard. Also on bills with Marty Wilde, Billy Fury, *Joe Brown, Terry Nelhams (aka Adam Faith) Wee Willie Harris, Duffy Power, Dickie Pride, Terry Dene.

Comment: *The above answer made so little mention of that tragic Gene and Eddie tour that I asked him to reflect in greater depth. This he later did, below. It makes for truly powerful reading. (Those with an asterisk against them have a separate Glossary entry in their name.)*

Answer No.2: Thinking of that last UK tour with Eddie and Gene saddens me to the core. Eddie inspired me with his wonderful guitar playing, which ranged from blues to jazz, encompassing everything in between. Standing in the wings and soaking up his performances with "dropped jaw" - and nothing but ears and eyes as he presented us young musicians with the perfect example of "how it should be done". He was the real thing, the authentic messenger in the service of the Lord, showing us the tools and demonstrating how to use them, all for the sake of, and in the name of freedom. Yes, freedom (and reconciliation, too).

Looking back, it's easy to see why souls like Eddie were sent. He was cast in the same mould as James Dean and Elvis, magnetic and pure magic, a species hitherto unknown. Sharon Sheeley, Eddie's girlfriend, used to conjure up visions of a typical musician's (rock 'n' roller's) life back in the States, especially in the Southern states where it all began... We kids listened, enthralled by Eddie's guitar picking in the dressing room (or on the tour bus), charmed out of our wits by the drawl and the body language of an authentic rocker at close quarters.

When Sharon talked of Elvis (with whom she was on the friendliest of terms) as if she'd only left him a couple of days prior it "rounded off" our image of him - at the same time hinting that Eddie was in no way a lesser phenomenon than Elvis. And didn't Eddie play "supremely good" guitar, whereas Elvis was the "ultimate showman". Back in the old days, all electric guitar strings were of the same gauge (e.g. Gibson "Sonomatic" strings). Eddie showed me how he by-passed the problem of too-heavy strings, and I quote: *"For the high E-string, you take a banjo string; for the B, you take an E regular; for the G, a B regular; for the D, a G regular..."* (and so on.) This system impressed me no end needless to say.

God, I'd have given almost anything to get a seat in the car taking Gene and Eddie from Bristol back to London on that last date of the tour in the Spring of 1960. Instead, for the first (and last) time in my life I purchased a half bottle of Scotch and proceeded to down it in the theatre dressing room. The unaccustomed whiskey, made me sick, so I smashed the half-empty bottle to smithereens against the dressing-room's brick wall, and retched my way back to the Bed 'n' Breakfast joint. The next morning we learned that Eddie was dead, the car having crashed not too far from Bristol. (Gene was hospitalised for some time to come).

Many years later, I asked Dave Dee why he didn't appear at the Chippenham Eddie Cochran Festival, as many of us have. He replied that on the fateful night he had been a Police Cadet on duty and was called to the accident scene shortly after the crash had happened. He said the horror had never left him…

Comment*: I'd speak with the late Dave Dee, about Tony, a few years ago and I'll recount one of his anecdotes later. (There's a biographical entry under both Eddie Cochran, Sharon Sheeley and Dave Dee in the Glossary section.)*

Question: *Any other memories from that fateful British tour with Eddie and Gene?*

Answer: Most of us were in crappy lodgings, eating crappy breakfasts, and the attitude was that you'd better be there or the tour bus would leave without you.

Comments: *I also recall Tony mentioning that (sadly) Gene was often drinking and his behaviour could be obnoxious. Seemingly a party-piece was to squeeze a person's neck till they momentarily became unconscious. Not something that endeared him to Tony or indeed any of the others!*

Question: *Do say something about your favourite guitar models.*

Answer: In the early years a preference for the Gibson ES-75 or the Martin D28-E. Later transition to solid bodies: Music Man, Strat. Always a fondness for lesser-known models, e.g. Martin GT-70. (Steinway of Hamburg, did a brisk trade in the '60s, supplying British musicians with "exotic" U.S. instruments).

Comment: *This answer is not at all unexpected. Tony's a legendary guitarist (The Teacher) and his opinions certainly demand respect.*

Question: *With the Vince Taylor group were you with the later Vince, or the early Vince, as I have video clips and you're not there.*

Answer: The gigs with Vince Taylor were sporadic and also not a labour of love. Formed mainly for the "Oh Boy!" show and his first single: "Right Behind You Baby". Vince concentrated on supplying a visual show a la Elvis, with a dash of Gene Vincent (leather and chains, etc.) - but this wasn't - musically speaking - my world at all. (My good mate Tony Harvey went on to play lead guitar with Vince when he moved to France, where he enjoyed a degree of popularity with the "noir" crowd).

Comment: *Vince Taylor (1939-1991) was actually born Maurice Holden in Britain but was brought up in the USA before returning to the UK and, as a leather-clad rocker, seeking his fortune here on the back of the rock 'n' roll explosion of the late '50s. He had some releases here but didn't break into the charts so emigrated to France where he had a successful early career before increasing health problems overtook him, and he died too early. But as Tony would say about his times with Vince, "I thought I was* *better", a view shared by the author. There's also a Glossary entry for Vince Taylor.*

Question: *Craig Douglas was (I believe) a big pal of the legendary Donald Campbell. Were there any unlikely figures that you have had links with? (I was aware that, in the late '50s, Craig Douglas had been signed to a record contract in preference to Sheridan.)*

Answer: Don't give a fig for *Craig Douglas connection with *Donald Campbell - must be the Scots blood, or something. Craig Douglas was the reason I never signed with the newly-formed record label: "Top Rank" in 1958/9! As he smiled more, they took him, rather than "fluffy haired" Tony Sheridan (author - the Melody Maker at one point reported that Tony was signing for Top Rank, briefly a prominent label during the late '50s.)

**Footnote:* Craig Douglas (born 1941 on the Isle of Wight) still performs and perhaps is best remembered for his 1959 UK No.1 "Only Sixteen", a cover of the Sam Cooke penned hit. (Most of his hits were in fact covers of US hits but that was very much a trend in that era.). Donald Campbell (1921-1967), a hero to the author, has no connection with music, but was the former British land and water speed record holder who captivated the British population for many years with his valiant exploits in the field of record-breaking. He sadly lost his life on Coniston Water while attempting to break his own record and go through the 300 mile per hour barrier. His body was not recovered until 2001.

Comment: *As can be seen Tony ignored the main thrust of the question but it did provoke a little insight as to how he nearly got signed up in the late '50s.*

Question: *I think they wanted you as a Shadow in the early years? (Note: they were, of course, to become The Drifters before morphing into Shadows.)*

Answer: The two Brians and I did back Cliff on a couple of occasions. Subsequently there may well have been an offer in sight. (Obviously, Cliff made them an offer they couldn't refuse!) In those days I was a wild man - Hank and Bruce were relatively docile chaps, and willing to back Cliff accordingly. For me that meant: "selling out" and a loss of personal integrity to boot. (There was a time when Paul Lincoln (2 I's) considered marketing me as Tony Sheridan - the Wild Man! No kidding).

Comment: *The two Brians are of course Bennett and Locking who were like Tony in London at the point as skiffling, rock 'n' roll wanabees. Interesting (above) to hear Tony be so totally honest about those days back then, when we have often read, from other sources, that for a while - before he made the move from London to Hamburg - he was his own worst enemy. Jack Good and others have said as much - it's an aspect that will be turned to again later.*

Question: *Did you play with Billy Fury/any Billy Fury anecdotes?*

Answer: Billy and I were occasionally on the same bill - mostly Parnes' one-nighters, but we never actually played together. We got on well.

Comment: *As mentioned earlier Tony and his trio were famously present throughout the final Eddie Cochran tour, and had to survive quite a bit of heckling too - something many of the British artists had to endure on such packages when Americans* *topped the bill. Incidentally, Billy Fury was on some of these Cochran/Vincent tour dates but not all. A contemporary of mine from the CNS remembers that fated tour well - he provided the following anecdote:*

*"The night we saw the show, Jan, 24th 1960 in Ipswich, the bill included Vince Eager, and at least one other British band (*author - *The Viscounts) and Tony Sheridan. Sheridan played lead guitar for Gene Vincent, accompanied by string bass and drummer. I seem to recall he played a Fender Stratocaster. TS also played rhythm behind Cochran, who was playing his 'usual' amplified non-solid bodied guitar, as per all the regular publicity shots and the famous The Girl Can't Help It film sequence. Vincent did a demonic set, togged out in head to toe leather, and urging Sheridan on to greater efforts in the guitar breaks while supporting his weight on the mike stand in his characteristic fashion to ease his damaged leg. I recall that in Cochran's set the American star suffered from amplifier gremlins, and took Sheridan's guitar from him for a couple of numbers."*

Question: *Did you meet any of the Crickets? (Forgive the author's indulgence having written about the group and met all of the main members, post-Buddy Holly.)*

Answer: Only Glenn D Hardin - but then he wasn't really a Cricket.

Comment: *Glenn was with the Crickets but intermittently. His lengthiest gigs (on keyboards) have been with both John Denver and Elvis Presley. Tony would later head up the TCB band of which Glenn was a member. (More of that later.)*

Question: *Did you play with Carl Perkins in the '60s?*

Answer: No. All young musicians of the 1950s/60s - especially guitarists and singers - respected Carl Perkins as one of the really authentic early rockers.

Comment: *The reader can perhaps guess that the author reveres the memory of the great musical pioneer Carl Perkins who he first saw on stage in Leicester back in 1964. (And the last time was to be in Lubbock, Texas in 1986).*

Question: *Did you ever go anywhere near any of the other '60s shows, e.g. Saturday Club with Brian Matthew on the BBC? (I appreciate that at this time you were probably gigging in Germany on the back of the success of "My Bonnie" with The Beatles).*

Answer: Might have... Never gigged on the back of any success - just built up a strong following based on respect and affection. "Success" was relative.

Comment: *An honest answer. I'm inclined to feel that TS has often passed up golden opportunities to further his career. As his answer implies he's probably been more ambitious to make music rather than make money. He also said to the author on another occasion: "I could have stayed and become a session guy but that wasn't me - I wanted to evolve, and progress my music" Knowing Tony he is being honest.*

Question: *I asked Tony about Gene's limp during that tour, as well as his deteriorating behaviour.*

Answer: Gene and Eddy were drinking more and more as the tour progressed and by the end they were just desperate to get home and be normal again ...Oh, and Gene was adamant that his leg problems arose when he was in the U.S. Navy and had been caused when some work involving the use of a high-pressure steam jet went wrong and caused the injuries.

Comment: *The second sentence is interesting. Gene told SO many stories concerning his leg problems back then but this seems the most likely of the ones the author has heard over the years.*

Question: *Aware that Tony had often met up with Gene in the '60s I asked whether he had any further reminiscences. (They made some appearances in Israel together during the course of the '60s.)*

Answer: Yes, I always felt that Gene was acting out the part of his image, you know? It seemed to me that he was always playing a part in a film. We'd always known that Gene didn't like playing night-clubs at all and cabaret audiences weren't his thing either. Sadly, Gene died the death that night (*author - at a gig in Israel*) - really there was no applause at all. Now whether it was because of his clothing and the whole imagery of wearing a medallion brought to the stage I don't know. Certainly in Europe and elsewhere rock 'n' roll was seen and understood for what it was but it certainly didn't travel to the Middle East back then. Later that night and for the rest of the gigs Gene was to drown his sorrows in the whiskey bottle - he simply could not understand why they did not like him.

Comment: *One wishes that the Gene Vincent story would have a happy ending, but it didn't and as we know he died of bleeding ulcers when just aged 36.*

...the crash which had cut short Cochran's life, had tragically altered Vincent's too, but had also profoundly affected many of those who were supporting the headliners on that last tour. And none more so than Tony who hadn't gone back to that interrupted limp-along rescheduled tour, headlined by Gene and propped up by others, instead as we know he'd continued to work wherever the offers came from. He no longer had any real ties with Larry Parnes, or selfish as it might seem, to anyone else for that matter. He needed to break away both musically and personally. Certainly by the time he'd decided to work in Germany, his short-lived and disastrous first marriage was already behind him. Caught up in the heady whirl of London and the whole entertainment scene when barely 18 years of age he'd fallen heavily for the charms of a young West End dancer named Hazel who he had first met when he was playing at the 2 1's Coffee Bar. Probably what happened thereafter can almost be guessed at - an unplanned pregnancy which would produce his first child Tony Sheridan junior, a "shot-gun wedding" (as he termed it) at a Registry Office, with future Shadows and pals Liquorice Locking and Brian Bennett acting jointly as his Best Men, and a relationship thereafter that would be measured more in weeks than months or years. He needed to get away....

CHAPTER 6 : ENTER THE BEATLES - PART ONE

"Shake it all day and shake it all night,
Shake it right now,
Hey shake it baby
Hey hey shake it baby"

"Shake It Some More". Composer - Tony Sheridan

BACK-STORY: Within a very few weeks of Tony's arrival (August, 1960) in the legendary Reeperbahn/St. Pauli district of Hamburg The Beatles would arrive to gatecrash the scene even if, initially, it had all started out somewhat depressingly for the group. Back then The Beatles were, of course, virtually unknown outside of Liverpool, having earned peanuts thus far, and had up to then been calling themselves The Silver Beatles. If their arrival in Germany was low key, they'd actually arrived squeezed into their manager's mini-bus, but like TS, they'd soon be attracting lots of attention as news of their riotous stage act spread. But surely Tony's earlier quote of being disgusted with the British scene circa 1960 is inadequate to explain the real reason as to why he moved abroad and, in doing so, bring about a such a volte-face in his life? The author wonders whether instead it was Tony's subconscious that had always been nagging away and steering him towards this end: call it fate if you prefer, but it certainly seemed as if destiny was waiting in the Hamburg wings for his arrival.

Alan Clayson's book, Hamburg: The Cradle of British Rock (see Bibliography) investigates the whole scene in Germany from the time of Sheridan's arrival and onwards into the '70s, and in far greater detail than is necessary here. But the reader needs to be reminded that it wasn't only Liverpool groups that had the monopoly in Hamburg back then, even if they had been well represented at the outset by Derry and the Seniors and Gerry and the Pacemakers . Of course Sheridan, from the backwaters of Norfolk, had helped to kick it all off, but soon afterwards a stream of groups from the Midlands, which would include Dave Dee, and elsewhere including the wider North East of England would follow before the bubble would inevitably burst. Meanwhile a selection of authentic American rock 'n' roll artists would also begin to make their way over the pond and include Germany on their tour itineraries: Ray Charles, Brenda Lee, Gene Vincent, Bill Haley and Jerry Lee were among several such musical tourists, even if for some their careers had already peaked, and their big pay-days were mostly in the past.

We'll go into Tony's Hamburg activities more in the next Chapter (Enter the Beatles: Part 2) but it would surely help if we first had the singer's thoughts on each of The Beatles as individuals, as well as a group, given that they'd just walked into each other's lives. So what follows next are some fairly potent comments on each of the various personalities. Even fans of the Fab Four might find some of these thoughts shed some new light onto the group's early years and how it was in the final days before they took the musical world by storm…

Please note that all the thoughts in this section are those of Tony, unless clearly indicated otherwise, and were given to the author via Fax messages from 2006 onwards.

Tony on John Lennon:

Well, when we met I kind of liked his caustic lip and secretly admired the Scouser "assuredness", and blatant, unmitigated abusiveness. He was rude, cruel, witty and unholy. I was, in a way, fortunate 'cause he liked me and - he respected, my creativity and musicianship. The Irish in him somehow recognised the Irish in me. He appreciated music, and held it to be a sacred gift of the Gods - which it is.

In recognising another authentic and genuine fellow aspirant, he was in a sense proving to himself that he was, too, one of the "chosen ones". ("It takes one to recognise another"). He felt validated, accepted, understood, appreciated, etc., by like-minded individuals. Music provided him with an identity that he considered to be more or less the real John - still in the formative stage, sure - but going somewhere that no-one else had ever been! His vehicle for personal growth and fruition was rock 'n' roll. He'd jumped on with skiffle music, and now he was well and truly married to his chosen art-form.

So in Hamburg he let it all hang out... As we all did, incidentally. And oh yes, he was the only guy I've seen with hairs growing out of the top of his nose. It was puzzling to me why he'd sometimes let them grow. There were about eight or ten of them, quite dark, too, like his eyebrows. (Author's interjection: *you'll see as the story progresses, and in line with his artistic nature, that Tony often seems drawn to mention some personal peccadillo. With Lennon the thought must surely arise: perhaps Shaved Nose rather than *Shaved Fish?)* At one time I was quite enamoured of his high-heeled suede boots, and as we had the same shoe-size, I asked if he would sell them to me - he could have the money at payday, and could I have the boots now? You must be joking, he said - no money, no boots!

**Footnote:* Shaved Fish being the title of Lennon's 1975 Greatest Hits compilation, a Top 10 album in the UK. A weak pun the author couldn't resist.

I never understood that attitude - but there again his main ambition (AD 1961) was to become rich. (Which for me didn't seem to fit in with playing music - at least, I was not able to view these two, conflicting, aspects together...) A bit later in life I surmised that for John finances meant primarily: freedom, i.e. - to live as someone who wants freedom, from convention, freedom to concentrate on furthering one's calling - to identify with a mission in life - (and freedom/exemption from being a "nowhere man".) The world loves and accepts an eccentric genius - but no-one loves or respects an eccentric idiot. John clearly saw that eccentricity only works in conjunction with creativity (=authentic originality).

Comment: *We know that John Lennon was definitely damaged by his childhood and would be left with unresolved issues. A musical genius perhaps but a flawed one. Or, perhaps as another musician interviewed by the author about those Hamburg days - not Tony - would say pungently when asked about Lennon: "John Lennon? He was a mean-spirited bastard!" Thankfully we won't let that be the final verdict but certainly it has to be said that he had many conflicting sides to his character and not all of them were exactly endearing. But Lennon, when recalling TS as "a performing legend" would also painfully recall those Hamburg days by saying that: "each song had to last 20 minutes and contain 20 solos!" Not literally true, but we do get the picture. And in a later letter that John would write in the '70s he mentions how good Sheridan was and how he knew exactly what the Germans' wanted. Flattering words indeed.*

Tony on Paul McCartney:

Paul is a Gemini ("quick-witted, versatile, innovative, etc.") So am I which meant that a degree of instant empathy - not necessarily sympathy - was present from the instant that we met. His cultured and somewhat effeminate outward appearance told me that here was a striving musician whose sensitivity would of necessity enrich anything he touched. He exuded a casual brightness, some of which you hoped would - like stardust - float over and settle on you, automatically endowing one with a dozen more musical facets.

Sitting down with Paul and two guitars would, within minutes, produce an idea for a song - or at least a title for a song that in itself suggested how a song with that title would probably turn out - the groove, the tempo, the phrasing of a line... A couple of years ago (*author - presumably circa 2004/5*) before a Hamburg concert, he remarked (in the dressing room) how well he remembered me perspiring on stage (he was cooler!), back in the "old days" when we performed every night for months on end... "You should write a song like this", he said strumming a couple of chords - and call it "Sweating Up a Storm"! I probably shall. I almost heard the completed song in my head when he said that. *(author: The only song Tony co-wrote with Paul was "Tell Me If You Can")*

Comment: *Being based abroad has also meant that TS has bumped into Paul infrequently in the years since their first meeting, but they have retained a friendship that is quickly rekindled every time their paths have crossed. And yes, Paul does sometimes teasingly use the title The Teacher in deference to the formal musical schooling of his friend. In fact in a newspaper interview in 2006 McCartney would look back and, in passing, make an oblique reference to Tony's musicality by stating: "We didn't know the rules. I remember in the very, very early days in Hamburg asking Tony Sheridan what he thought of one of our songs, and Tony said 'Well, it's just a scale!'" Of course, to Tony that's the way his musical mind has always worked, and still does now. And Paul, although famously not having had much formal musical training, hasn't let that prove a hindrance to his musical outpourings over the years.*

And there is another anecdote that the author recalls TS telling him. It was in the late '60s when the Beatles had achieved super-stardom and Tony was in London and in his cups that he and a fellow-musician decided to make an unannounced visit to Macca's London home - perhaps not a good idea. Clambering over a neighbour's fence they eventually arrived at Paul's door and Linda let them in. Tony was adamant he wanted to show Paul a "weird chord" only to frustratingly find that Paul could only find a left-handed guitar! All in all a rather ignominious visit one feels. Tony will talk again about Paul again while reflecting about George, below. Oh, and it's a very minor point but both Macca and Tony share the fact that they come from parents with differing religious backgrounds, one of whom was Catholic whilst the other was a Protestant.

Tony on George Harrison:

The 'chemistry' of the "complete" Beatles naturally included George's artistic contribution, which was of course, spiritual in nature. Exactly how their combined energies functioned, has yet, in theory, to be fathomed, (although, possibly it is unfathomable). George acted as the catalyst between John and Paul (with Ringo as the "regulator" or "stabiliser"). Obviously, a good drummer needs to be these - he was these also in a higher sense.

For all his young years, George was an amazingly stable character. (Today I would use the term "an old soul".) Slow in speech and actions, soft and underfed in appearance, (as many of us were!), thoughtful and considerate… and obsessed with playing guitar! He told me he had watched me "on the box" (the "Oh Boy!" shows), and that I, as well as others, was partly responsible for his having decided to become a musician. (George even went as far as to get himself a "FUTURAMA" guitar because I had played one on TV.) On another occasion, he confided that there had, in effect, been no 'decision' at all - rather, life itself did the deciding. As I was into "weird chords", he expressed a great interest in acquiring a working knowledge of "alternative harmonies".

Doubtless, his musical knowledge and ideas were duly incorporated into the Beatles' combined oeuvre, and expressed in dabs and doses throughout their arrangements. (When I first heard the intro to "Come Together", it was immediately clear to me where the D minor seventh had originated.) With the arrival of the Fender bass, many bass players were tempted to "play too many notes" thus defeating the real issue of providing a rather solid rhythm basis of predominantly deep notes. As the bass part, and bass as an accompanying instrument are so important to me as a musician, I have always been a stickler for "real" bass playing. "Paul, please play like a real bassist you know, lots of low notes - and stay on the same note more often…" Which Paul does do on e.g. "Come Together".

On "My Bonnie" I distinctly remember asking him to play mainly a low C note on the second part of the guitar solo. It's amazing how effective this sort of playing can be. The Beatles' recordings are adequate proof that Paul played bass "as bass should be played"! Jack Bruce with Cream, featuring Eric Clapton and Ginger Baker, was not so steadfast! Cream, comprising three soloists on their individual trips didn't make for an especially cohesive trio. Jimi Hendrix, on the other hand, made sure his bassist and drummer "toed the line" - and his concept functioned extremely well.

Comment: *Decidedly the youngest of all the Beatles, George was born in 1943, and seems to have been the one that Tony remembers with the most affection: "he was so young, so shy". Shortly after George's death Tony released an album Vagabond, dedicated to the singer's memory, the inner sleeve of which featured the two men together, in affectionate pose, arms draped around one another's shoulders. And George Harrison would personalise it when he said: "All I know about rock 'n' roll, I learned from Tony Sheridan". Not a bad quote for someone to have on their CV.*

Also and to this day, in the absence of George, a McCartney greeting for TS might well be, "Got any new weird chords?" And as Tony readily admits, "instead of three chords I'd often play ten!" TS would also tell the author at one point, "My interest in playing 'weird chords' where there were otherwise none , helped bring a little diversity into playing the same old three-chord rock 'n' roll songs ad nauseam." Of course, George was to later get into weird chords extensively. In a biography of Harrison by Marc Shapiro the latter quotes TS as saying: "George in particular was a literal sponge during those sessions soaking up the atmosphere and the studio vibe. He was very keen on learning anything he could. He was not looked upon by the others as being particularly good, although they liked his image and the way he stood in the background. Of course he wanted to be more in the forefront but felt he could only do it by improving his knowledge."

Tony on Pete Best

Pete and I had our (mostly musical) differences, to be sure. The other Beatles and Pete also had theirs, which were a little more obtuse. But there's more to it than that. Pete's style of drumming lacked a heavy driving backbeat - in fact, so did most drummers of that epoch; and this was especially true of Merseyside drummers. The popular style of drumming on the Liverpool scene was - well, to my mind - a bit insipid. As is the case with all musicians, one is influenced by one's model; but at that time there were (in Britain) very few "red-hot" drummers to speak of.

But it was precisely this lack of an offbeat that urged John and Paul to overcome this problem - to compensate, by assuming as it were, the responsibility for a solid and compact rhythm section! In one sense - and this may sound a bit far-fetched - Pete was something of a martyr. Had he performed as a competent and convincing drummer from the start, then the others, particularly John and Paul, would not have developed their musical style as it gradually emerged in Hamburg. The fact that Paul played bass "like a bassist" also contributed much to the overall feel typified by much of the Beatles' later music. ("Lady Madonna", "Back in the USSR", "Get Back" - but also ballads, e.g. "Golden Slumbers".)!

Ringo having also been conditioned in my band to put down, amongst other things, a strong heavy off-beat and to play clear-cut, pithy fill-ins, immediately complemented Paul's bass style. Both musicians attitudes originated from a common source, and were thus easily compatible. To put it more succinctly - they had gone through the same (hard) school! (These days I can unabashedly reconcile myself to the theory sometimes put forward, namely, that performing with Tony Sheridan for any length of time will make, or break, a budding musician. That some of them were extremely talented, becoming famous and "bigger than Jesus", is by the way...)

Comment: *This answer above, like so many by Tony, starts off addressing the specific subject matter (Pete Best) but, towards the end of his ruminating he's moved off somewhere else. But at least by leaving it 'as written' and un-amended the reader can hopefully follow his train of thought. Tempting as it may be for the author to try to abridge, amend or switch parts of answers to a different, ostensibly more appropriate header, it would clearly be misleading.*

Question: *But before we leave Pete Best I had to ask him about the marathon fight he and Best had one night after one of their Club gigs and he basically confirmed the way it had first been reported in the '60s and as it's set out below. It seems Tony had been pestering him to play some particular arrangement of his (Tony's) on drums but Pete insisted that he preferred to do things in his own way. Evidently TS droned on endlessly about it and ended up telling Best he must play it Tony's way, or else! The bluff having been called the two antagonists duly squared up outside the club at the end of the night.*

Answer: Pete and I had been arguing musical policy for some time and it had come to a head that night. We stopped playing in the middle of a number and prepared for a punch-up. The audience were yelling and goading us on. But we didn't scrap until after the club was closed. Down a dark alley we had a physical argument which lasted for about two hours and at the end of it Pete and I were the best of friends. (This was basically the way he described it to the NME back in 1964.)

Comment: *But note that although they had a running fist fight that went on for hours (or so it seemed) and ended up with both men bloody there were to be no long term differences and both men would meet up again 20 years on in the San Fernando Valley, near Los Angeles where Sheridan was then living, reminiscing about those Hamburg days and in particular their extraordinary fight. There's a short entry on Pete Best in the Glossary.*

Tony on Ringo Starr

When the Beatles and George Martin decided to drop Pete Best, Ringo was ready to fill the slot, having been waiting "in the wings", so to speak. Going back to the time in the Top Ten Club when I had to form another "Beat Bros", (after the Beatles engagement at the club with myself) Ringo seemed to me to be the only likely candidate-for-drummer around. Peter Eckhorn (boss of the Top Ten) and I drove through the night to Liverpool, where I knocked on Ringo's door and asked him to come back to Hamburg for a longish gig at Peter's club, with Roy Young and myself in the band. *(Author - in fact Tony and The Jets opened Eckhorn's club The Top Ten, a converted Hippodrome on the Reeperbahn, in the August of 1960. Both the Beatles and Sheridan would bunk down in the attic premises above the club - facilities were said to be nil).*

Now Ringo really had to suffer torments as we put him through the ropes, forming his playing style into what we expected of him, as the drummer in our band. It brought out the "slumbering" Ringo (and the best in him). He may have moaned now and then on stage at some of my "creative arrangements" (the "longer" ones) - but when the gig finished a couple of months later, he'd become very proficient and had much more expertise, in a wider musical sense, than prior to our mutual collaboration.

When I knocked on his family's terrace house door in Liverpool, he of course had no inkling of what was yet to come. (Neither did I, for that matter!) Previously we had had little personal contact. He was "one of the Scousers", and a bit of a belated Teddyboy, too. Just a little "out of sync" as far as his appearance was concerned. He'd told me about his childhood history of lengthy periods of hospitalisation due to acute rheumatic fever, and other complications. All of which kept him out of school and mostly in bed. An early life of deprivation of all kinds. Wish I could have been engaged by the relevant angel folks to inform Ringo of his later-in-life gig in my band, and to break the news that he was destined to become the drummer of the biggest, most famous and most successful group of all time! Alas, this role was denied me. Still, in retrospect it makes for a very pleasant, little story, and I am the only one qualified to tell it this way, from his angle. I only regret never having enquired of Ringo why one of his eyebrows and a streak in his hair were white. He had very white teeth to match... *(Author: yet another example of Tony being drawn to quirky personal characteristics.)*

Comment: *As Beatles fans will know it was in 1962 when Ringo finally joined the Fab Four and replaced Pete Best, having also been part of Tony's backing group for some two months during that same year. (As we all know Pete Best was badly affected by his exit from the Beatles and was so low that at one point that he came very close to committing suicide.)*

Tony on Stuart Sutcliffe

Stuart was a talented painter, a pleasant chap, a deep thinker, a lousy bass player… and, an important catalyst for the Beatles. Though Paul would have had a problem with this appraisal of Stuart's role as a Beatles "compadre" they were, essentially, anathema to one another. Stuart and John shared a deep affection (if nothing further).

Had Stuart been a talented bass player, then John would certainly have opted for him as the Beatles' official bassist. Fortunately for Paul, Stu's talent lay in other spheres… (All of which is not to say that John and Paul would not have gone on to write (and sing) great (Beatle) songs!) As it happened, Paul took over the role of bass player himself - almost overnight - learning (teaching himself) to both play the bass and sing simultaneously (which is not easily mastered; many cannot manage it at all).

TS would also make the point to Stuart Sutcliffe's sister Pauline that perhaps he (Stuart) was playing the wrong instrument. Tony explains it thus: It looked very strange, this small chap with an amazingly big bass. Stuart wasn't really a guitarist or a singer, and he obviously wasn't a drummer. Maybe today, with all the technological possibilities, he would have found a way. But I feel his involvement was that of a catalyst. He wasn't interested in being in the limelight as a musician. He was more interested in being a part of that in a roundabout way, on the periphery.

Comment: *In a later chapter describing those epic Hamburg recording sessions with The Beatles Tony mentions that the regular bassist Stuart Sutcliffe had pulled out in the weeks running up to the session having passed his actual bass guitar to Paul. (Interestingly Stuart Sutcliffe, although not involved in the recordings, was to send a copy of the "My Bonnie" single to his sister in England remarking rather cryptically that it wasn't as good as it could have been, although he didn't elaborate as to exactly why!) Hopefully he shared in the excitement that all of them would have felt - actually getting to appear on a record. An extremely big deal for all concerned. Certainly Stuart had a moody stage persona and on the few onstage photos of that time he almost seems to have his back turned to the audience - it has also been said rather unkindly that this was primarily to hide the fact he would occasionally chose the wrong key to play in! It seems certain that he was always destined to struggle musically, particularly when playing alongside such amazingly talented colleagues.*

One suspects that it's quite a challenge for anyone who isn't a natural musician to play the bass. Bandleader Howie Casey, whose band Stuart also occasionally played with in Hamburg, is quoted as saying that as a bassist Stuart needed to stay within a strict twelve-bar blues formula, while George Harrison would also reflect on his friend's bass playing abilities by saying laconically: "it was better to have a bass player that couldn't play rather than no bass player". If that would seem to damn Stuart with faint praise few have ever sought to discredit his talents on the wider artistic front, and no doubt helped by his Beatles links his artwork has become increasingly sought after as the years have gone on. (See Glossary for a brief entry on Stuart Sutcliffe.)

…having heard some of Tony's thoughts about the various members of the Beatles we now move on to look at the time he played the Hamburg clubs and in using his words we'll hear a bit more about John, Paul, George, Ringo, Stuart, Pete (and even Brian Epstein) and what went on during that rather special time. Did Tony take drugs back then - he's temporarily incandescent when this is put to him, as you'll shortly read…

CHAPTER 7 : ENTER THE BEATLES - PART 2

"I played my game with every girl I met
Gave her my money but she wanted my mind
I done so many things I can't forget
Landed me in trouble 'bout a hundred times"

Sinkin' Composer - Tony Sheridan

BACK-STORY: We heard briefly in the previous chapter that Tony arrived in Hamburg during the summer of 1960 but we need to know more. The tale is usually told of how Bruno Koschmider, a Hamburg Club owner, had originally been recommended to try his luck in Liverpool, in some ways the British equivalent of Hamburg, but en route would stop off in London and end up in the heart of Soho. Thereafter as fate would have it he apparently bumped into an itinerant Scottish musician and friend of Sheridan's, Iain Hines, who enterprisingly recommended the services of an unnamed group of which he (Hines) and Tony just happened to be the nucleus! Just as quickly a name, The Jets, was instantly conjured up and TS, who was apparently present when all this was being worked out, was the obvious choice to front the newly-minted outfit.

So just who were the remaining Jets that were about to head off into the unknown back in 1960. Well, initially it would be Tony Sheridan and Rick Richards (aka Rick Hardy) who acted as vocalists with Tony's pal Colin Wilander on stand-up bass along with a second bass guitarist, Pete Wharton. Tony's pal Rick would also often share the mike and, it's a little known fact, was actually signed by Bert Kaempfert and made a Polydor single for German release fully six months or so before Bert approached TS. Sadly Rick was to die a few years ago in a German car crash and is much missed by his many musical pals. Del Ward, which was an alias, was next enlisted as the group's drummer and would sign the Hamburg contract for them all as Band Leader using the name of James Macken. Ironically, the only one who wasn't able to travel to Germany at the outset was Iain Hines (who, incidentally, was the brother of actor Fraser Hines) who'd helped to set the whole thing up. And so it came about that a gaggle of musicians would eventually make their meandering way to Hamburg, somewhat slowly via ferry, train and with the odd delay thrown in. Incidentally, Chas McDevitt, in a recent interview on those early days would say unequivocally that Tony Sheridan and The Jets were the first rock group to go to Germany - an interesting if debateable statistic. Now back to Tony.

Question: *Did you first meet the Beatles in September, 1960 in Hamburg? (It hadn't taken long for Welsh-born Liverpool coffee bar owner Allan Williams to link up with Bruno Koschmider and agree that the then unknown Beatles, who had been loitering in his own backyard, should try the same Hamburg trail as Sheridan. All that was needed was to get a bit of paperwork sorted out in a hurry and The Beatles would begin the long drive across France towards Germany.)*

Answer: After our initial gigs at the Kaiserkeller (August 1960) in the St. Pauli district, we (The Jets) played briefly at a quasi-strip club called Studio X while we were waiting to move to the bigger Top Ten club which was being decorated in readiness. It was there - in the middle of playing Buddy Holly's 'Not Fade Away' - that I remember The Beatles wandering in intent on grabbing some of that Sheridan stuff, by which I mean the music of course! That was to be the start of it all and some of the most wonderfully gratifying musical sessions I have ever experienced with the Beatles took place in those clubs in Hamburg. There were many such occasions but frustratingly not one single evening was ever recorded! But the thing to remember about being on stage was that it was a seven hour a night thing and so it either made you good or else you packed up. I remember George telling me early on that he'd brought over a guitar like the one he'd seen me playing on the "Oh Boy!" television show. It was a rubbish guitar, a Futurama I believe and was really a copy of a Fender. By this time I'd got rid of mine and was into real guitars; Gibson's. But that does show how obsessed George was with what I was doing at the time. *(Author - Tony had made the same point earlier re George and the guitar.)*

Comment: *Years later Tony would record a live version of "Not Fade Away" at The Star Club. But what was weird was, in contrast to the Vincent/Cochran tour when he'd hammered his way through say three numbers, suddenly he had to stretch his turn at the mike into a session that could last anything up to seven, even eight hours. The hours were crazy and would remain so, while the pay was not exactly generous. It's also worth adding that mention of the Reeperbahn/St. Pauli might dazzle the reader but the area was, in effect, a conglomeration of clip joints and, as a port, was geared to the many seamen which the area attracted.*

Question: *Elvis being in Germany 1958/60. Relevant to you? (But of course I should have anticipated the answer)*

Answer: When we arrived, he'd left.

Comment: *Oops, silly question. But I thought that maybe their tenure had just overlapped - in fact Elvis was discharged as a Buck Sergeant (that's the most junior ranking Sergeant) on March 5th, 1960.*

Question: *Did you know all of the Beatles equally well.*

Answer: As well as you can know anyone, when one is in the same boat, sailing to somewhere distant and exotic, and hoping the boat would not fall off the edge if the Earth proved to be flat after all!

Comments: *Tony has never been less than laudatory about the (Beatles) group that he was to be thrown together with in Germany. It was a magical time for him, although he could never have anticipated what was to follow.*

Question: *What about the rooming arrangements at the Bambi Kino (Hamburg club)? Any memories?*

Answer: Never played or slept there. I heard the sleeping arrangements were pretty bad. The Beatles were not exactly enamoured of their "quarters" there. But there again, back in those days nobody saw us as human beings with sensitive souls! St. Pauli wasn't Greenwich Village, either. Soho had been closer.

Comment: *The Bambi-Filmkunsttheatre, or the Bambi Kino as it was popularly known, lacked the charm of the Disney character from which it had obviously taken its name and was in fact a cinema whose staple fare in the '60s was primarily B movies of distinctly varying quality.*

LOU REED

MY BONNIE
TONY SHERIDAN AND THE BEAT BROTHERS
STEREO
Tony Sheridan
MY BONNIE · SKINNY MINNY · WHOLE LOT OF SHAKIN' GOING ON · I KNOW BABY
YOU ARE MY SUNSHINE · READY TEDDY · THE SAINTS · HALLELUJAH, I LOVE HER SO
LET'S TWIST AGAIN · SWEET GEORGIA BROWN · SWANEE RIVER · TOP TEN TWIST

MOSS'
EMPIRE
GLASGOW
Theatre
6-25 MON. FEBRUARY 1st 8-40
LARRY PARNES presents
TWO SENSATIONAL AMERICAN STARS !
FIRST EVER VISIT TO BRITAIN
GENE VINCENT
AND THE
FABULOUS WILDCATS
(By kind permission of MARTY WILDE)
YOUR HOST AND COMPERE
BILLY RAY
THE
Pye Disc Artistes
VISCOUNTS
TONY SHERIDAN TRIO
FROM I.T.V.'S 'OH BOY'

polydor
TONY SHERIDAN

SAINTS

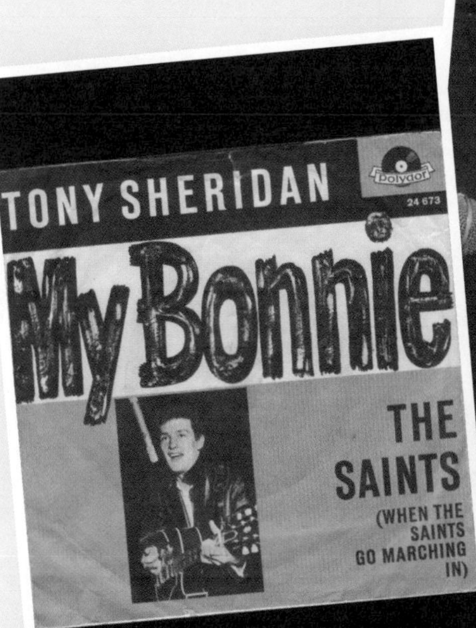
TONY SHERIDAN
Polydor
24 673
My Bonnie
THE SAINTS
(WHEN THE SAINTS GO MARCHING IN)

MUSICIANS
HALL of FAME
& MUSEUM
NASHVILLE

MISTER
TWIST
TONY
SHERIDAN
WHEN THE SAINTS
CRY FOR A SHADOW
MY BONNIE
WHY
21 914 Médium

polydor

Question: *What about 'drugs'? A recent Beatles book (this question was posed in 2006) suggested you were a major provider. Or do you want to ignore the subject? (Another question calculated to get the Sheridan hackles to rise!)*

Answer: Once and for all - the suggestion that I was ever a "(major) provider" of drugs is so utterly preposterous (and insulting) that words almost fail me. And who wants to "ignore the subject"?! You give me no choice but to defend myself and my integrity by being completely open (even to attack so it seems).

The so-called "suppliers" were the toilet-ladies. This means that they made a profit by selling Preludin pills to anybody. One pill cost 50 *Pfennig (when the £ was worth approx. 10DM). A whole tube cost approximately three *Deutsche Mark at the chemist's shop. The pills were legal, but only on prescription. Certain criminal elements from St. Pauli obtained large amounts of Preludin by breaking into chemists. We musicians occasionally used the "pill" to stay awake. The work was both physically and mentally exhausting to the point of collapse. One hour's stage work was equivalent to several hours of physical labour... Ask anyone who did it what that really meant ! As the pills deprived us of sleep, there was no question of using them on a regular basis. But on a Saturday night... well, it happened.

**Footnote:* Before the advent of the Euro the German currency was the Mark, which comprised 100 Pfennig.

Other than "Prellies" we used no other drugs at all - legal or otherwise. No "grass", no "pot", (and certainly no "heavy" substances). As I've said before, a stint in the St. Pauli clubs meant, essentially: 80% music, 15% personal contacts, (inc. food) and 5% beer! The notion of "sex 'n' drugs 'n' rock 'n' roll" ever having been a musician's reality in Hamburg was (is) ludicrous. As far as I can ascertain, the phrase (and what it entailed) was coined by the media. It probably originated in "swinging" London of the '60s... Carnaby Street and what have you. As with many such "verbal banners", it was (is) grossly exaggerated. Sensation sells, as we all know. T Rex and the Rolling Stones may have profited from "hip" publicity, and contributed to the myth surrounding the pop-star glamour and glitter period. These days nobody really cares re: who does what - and anyway, junkies are definitely not "in". (Incidentally, more drugs were circulating in Vietnam than in the whole of the rest of the "civilized" world!)

Comment: *To repeat, an American author, I forget exactly who, had recently described Sheridan as the Johnny Appleseed of drugs back in those Hamburg days. Tony was briefly apoplectic at the slur. And I'm sure it was mostly alcohol back then, and a phrase of Tony's has stayed in my mind, "Look, after 15 beers one was less likely to fall off stage!"*

Question: *Another author has criticised you for dodging from number to number and leaving backing musicians bemused, and taking a "wanton" disregard, etc. etc. (I did name the writer and give Tony the exact quotes). Is this fair comment and why did you sometimes do this?*

Answer: "Dodging from number to number"? Well, on occasion certain musicians (not regular band members!) were confused and obviously unable to think clearly/adapt to the situation . Roy Young may have been confused on occasions.

John, Paul, George and Ringo hardly ever. (I was a stickler for good solid groove, tempo and musicality. Oh yes!) John certainly appreciated the "good training" - Paul, too. George lapped it all up. Ringo - well, it took a while to wake him up to his own possibilities… St. Pauli was the Academy of Rock and Applied Rhythm 'n' Blues. And the Beatles did ask me to go back with them! His *(the un-named author's)* use of the word "wanton" says more about him than me. (Wanton = (1) Causing harm or damage deliberately and for no acceptable reason (2) Behaving immorally : Oxford Dictionary. Dedicated I was. (But "wanton dedication"?!)

Strangely, most of my colleagues - past and present - were lavish in their praise and admiration for my work. This can get to be a bit embarrassing sometimes. Constructive criticism is always welcome, but he (*the un-named author again*) does tend to bend the facts (and the language, too). He does seem a bit bemused on occasion - (I shall have to speak to him). Where does he get his information from?

Comment: *Tony can get quite agitated about authors/critics etc. It's rather surprising he didn't get more agitated with me but I suppose that having (literally) tangled in the Infants school playground at five years of age acts as a great leveller. The author asked him to explain about joining the Beatles and all he would say was, "Look. I never wanted that. I was in love and happy in Hamburg for the moment so had no interest whatsoever in going back to London".*

Question: *Did you have special empathy with John and Stu because of the art work link. (As the reader will recall Tony was briefly an art student when back in Norwich.)*

Answer: "Arty" (in the positive sense, which includes folk who appreciate art, further its various forms, or inspire others) and artistic people seem to attract one another; and when they do make contact, it often happens spontaneously, dispensing with social formalities, for which they have little use… Johnny Gustafson, a bass player from Liverpool (The Big Three) introduced himself to me by burping in my ear and saying something like: "Good one, tonight, Sheridan…" And John L would sometimes approach another musician, and with his forefinger deep in his nostril, proceed to open a conversation, say, about Chuck Berry. (John liked to shock others with his irrational behaviour!)

Comment: *Tony here gives a somewhat esoteric answer to what was meant to be a straightforward question.*

Question: *Did you ever meet up with Brian Epstein?*

Answer: I met him on several occasions - in Hamburg (when John Lennon, as an affectionate gesture, no doubt, poured a large beer over Brian's head. Brian took it in his stride, presumably understanding it as it was doubtless meant.) More notably, with George Harrison in London at Brian's flat, around '63 or '64(?) (don't remember exactly: but George had just taken possession of a new Jaguar "E-type" (red) - which he later crashed…) I had been to Savile Row (Apple) to see the boys. As I recall, *"Creedence" was "in" and popular at their office. Apparently, Ringo, especially loved their music.

**Footnote:* Creedence Clearwater Revival, with John Fogerty on lead vocals, were one of the best American bands of that time, their music being almost a throwback to the rock ‘n’ era of the ’50s.

Anyway, I had just summoned up enough gall, or whatever, to ask Brian if he was perhaps interested in doing something “constructive” for me. (I knew he appreciated me and my role in bringing him and the Beatles together.) He told me that he was hopelessly busy with his “other” acts, i.e. Gerry Marsden, Tommy Quickly, etc., and I believed him, too. My impression was that he had way too much “on his plate”. However, he did ask me if I would agree to Gerry recording one of my songs: “Please Let Them Be”. Of course, I said yes. Brian really believed he was obliged to assist me in some way or other. George had suggested to Brian that Gerry do the song, and Brian listened, and liked it, too. So Gerry recorded it but it didn’t do too much… But he did quite a good job of singing it.

Comment: *The single was put out under Gerry Marsden’s solo name rather than as by Gerry and the Pacemakers. This came just after Gerry’s huge run of success as a group but the momentum had dissipated and the moment had gone.*

Question: *Your opinion please on some outlandish stuff, e.g. like Epstein/Lennon had affair, or whether Epstein was murdered.*

Answer: If the episode featuring the beer-pouring meant anything intimate, then I guess they were fond of each other! Regarding Brian’s demise… who knows? There are some really evil people in this world, of that I have no doubt.

Comment: *The Beatles manager, who died of an accidental drugs overdose shortly after signing (in 1967) a further five year deal with the Beatles, left a vacuum and a complex situation that was to create many problems over the ensuing years, and as the group eventually split in 1970, it’s sometimes interesting to speculate on what would have happened if he’d still been their manager.*

Question: *The whole Epstein family story seems sad. Brian’s brother Clive, for example, died within months of their mother.*

Answer: Does tragedy “balance out” extreme good fortune?… Seems likely - at least in some cases.

Comment: *The unspoken word ‘karma’ is lying at the back of this question and is implied in Tony‘s answer. We’ll come to the spiritual side of Tony’s life shortly.*

Question: *Did you know Mal Evans, the former Road Manager of the Beatles who was shot dead in the USA in the 1970s.*

Answer: No - didn‘t know Mal Evans personally.

Question: *Rory Storm. Any thoughts? (Of course, most Beatles fans will know of Rory’s name and know that Ringo was a drummer with his group pre-Beatles.)*

Answer: Rory, poor old soul. In those days it was not easy to be gay. They’d get beat up by morons, and worse. The good thing about Rory was: he got over his stuttering speech BY SINGING! Sounded great. (I once offered to swap my Martin electric for his Fender Strat. He refused, so sod him).

Comment: *Knowing Tony’s ironic turn of humour hopefully that story is told with affection.*

Question: *Did you meet the Beatles again after the 1961/62 Hamburg interlude? I read of you meeting George and Ringo after the Hard Day's Night film. True? Any other times?*

Answer: The last time we met up when all (*but see later correction below*) of the Beatles were present was in '64 on a BOAC (or was it a Quantas?...) 'plane bound for Australia. That is, I was flying "down under" while they were getting off in Manila, I think it was. (You would have to check this, though I'm pretty sure of the time/place scenario.). The boys invited me to sit with them in the first-class seating area, and a party ensued. John's Aunt Mimi was there, as well as assorted members of the Beatles' "entourage". Correction: Ringo was not well and had been replaced by drummer Jimmy Nicol. Jimmy and I had known each other well from the London SOHO scene of the late '50s, and we had often performed together. Co-incidence? Hardly, I should venture - NOTHING happens purely by chance or "co-incidence". (Still, some round-about connections do seem a bit "creepy"!). John and I were never to meet again... Regrettably.

Comment: *The author has no pretensions of being a Beatles anorak so has made no attempt to try and correct any of Tony's answers. Those who look for minutiae are welcome to do so.*

Question: *About more recent times what is your opinion about the take-off of you in the Backbeat film? And what is your general opinion of such take-offs?*

Answer: Never saw the film - probably never shall. No interest in lukewarm dish-ups of the period - I experienced first hand. Films never get it right anyway.

Comment: *Given the film concentrates on the Stuart Sutcliffe 'angle' the treatment of Tony Sheridan (in the author's opinion) is nothing short of derisory. Jurgen Vollmer - who wasn't even mentioned in the film - would, a few years ago, describe it as totally unauthentic and totally boring.*

Question: *Were you The Teacher to all? I assume just the guitar toting ones. (Since asking this question I've stumbled on the fact that jazz sax legend John Coltrane called Miles Davis The Teacher - so Tony's in excellent company!)*

Answer: Where does the "Teacher" expression originate? What does it mean? Certainly, there were a few licks and chords that I was able to pass on to fellow guitarists. More important, as I recall, was the ability to inspire others to greater things. This sounds perhaps too grandiose - but in practice, I took great personal delight in bringing out the best in us all.

The ostensible reason for playing in a band (group) on stage was to be seen and heard, and earning some money (if only a pittance!) in the process. The less apparent exercise was; to do it well, which included a string of other conscious or unconscious factors. Firstly, it became almost inevitable that "experimental playing" (as opposed to "improvisation") became the unspoken order of the day. This usually entailed elongating a song in its duration from, say, 2min 30secs ("like the record in the jukebox") to anything up to 15 minutes or more! This could be managed in different ways...

Repeating verses, varying the tempo, introducing additional breaks (stops), changing the "feel" of a number (e.g. from *"white" to "black"). A favourable method was - in any given piece - to give each band member a solo during which the others refrained from playing. Now and again, when it came to the drummer's turn, the rest of us would leave him to it and go to the bar for a "sojourn". (We'd try to be back within ten minutes or so!). As I recollect, it was mainly at my instigation that "experimental playing" came into being. The long, long hours required of us daily provided the backdrop on which we could experiment. The "Masters of Innovation" might have been a good name for a group - (compare with **"Mothers of Invention").

**Footnote:* Tony is using this terminology to differentiate the predominantly (white) pop style from the more rhythmic (rhythm and blues) style.

***Footnote:* Eclectic US group formed by Frank Zappa (1940-1993) who were most well-known for a series of hit albums in the early '70s with titles such as Burnt Weeny Sandwich and Weasels Ripped My Flesh.

The "fine art of experimental playing" had other, finer, connotations too. One was "chemistry". Good chemistry in a band produced music that was more of a sum of its components. (Strangely, one could hate a group member but at the same time produce "wonderful chemistry" with him in musical interaction.) An even finer, though rarer, form of creative interaction was essentially telepathic in nature. Then in the most rare cases of all, communion of a spiritual nature takes place between two or more musicians. This can, of course, include an audience too. This is akin to a religious experience - which it no doubt is, in a wider sense than if it were restricted to a particular belief or religious system.

In fact, any form of art can communicate an almost divine inspirational quality, (as a transmitter to a receiver), or trigger a spiritual experience. Some of the most wonderfully gratifying musical sessions I have ever experienced, (for instance, with the Beatles) took place in a club in Hamburg. There were many such occasions. Not one single evening was ever recorded!!!

Comment: *If one answer illustrates how seriously Tony takes his music it is surely evident here. Plus, it also illustrates a major frustration - witness the final sentence - that there is so little to show for his protracted involvement with John and Paul and the others from those Hamburg years, apart from the odd on-stage photo and the Hamburg recordings. Of course Tony had grown up back in Norwich playing a battered guitar and he'd often reverted to using his violin (when fronting The Saints) if it added to the overall feel. And he'd use the violin in any way possible, and that included playing it pizzicato and held high on his chest, guitar-style. Did this distinctive approach, which surely carried itself on to Hamburg, help influence John Lennon's own guitar-toting style? Who knows, everybody was influencing everybody or else making it up as they went along. Iain Campbell of The Big Six (the group who often backed TS in Germany) felt that Tony's guitar style was more energetic than anyone's and in fact as a result Sheridan would at one point accidentally acquire a broken finger to help prove the point!*

Question: *Did you know Astrid Kirchherr (Stu Sutcliffe's intended) very well? Knowing you from years ago I assume you must have lusted after her.*

Answer: In her way, she (as, indeed were all the other befriended art-school students) was essential to the "Top Ten scene", a motley lot of contrasting personalities, all of them important ingredients in the "cake" that comprised a typical night's audience. Did she realise - quite early on - that she was ordained to act as a catalyst for several talented individuals simultaneously? I think not. However, she did personify the main female element - the anima perhaps - in a tightly-knit self-appreciation club. In other words, she was aware that just her presence in our group presented the other key members with a degree of self-esteem which we wouldn't otherwise have acknowledged in ourselves. Astrid, Klaus, Jurgen and others succeeded in convincing us that our wayward musical meanderings constituted a valid art form - (with sophisticated eyes and ears) - they saw and heard us as such!

Previously even the more creative "rock" musicians among the British creative crowd that emerged in the late fifties considered themselves somewhat tainted by the negative image imposed on us by a conservative British society. It was good and reassuring to be accepted by likeminded, and obviously kindred, souls. In a word - they said YES, PLEASE to our still early, faltering steps to burst out of our shells. To say that Astrid was a "mother hen" would not be too far removed from the actual truth... And within the confines of our individual hearts, each of us black-leathered pseudo-rockers was reduced to adolescent courtier status. That we were also more than a bit mystified goes without saying. And perhaps, this was our first (mutual) encounter with what is often referred to as "platonic" love.

Comment: *Tony's answer well and truly put the author in his place with a deep and structured reply to what was a somewhat frivolous question. (Rather than digress here there's more on Astrid Kirchherr and several of her artistic Germans contemporaries in the Appendix towards the end of the book.)*

Question: *Tony, what was it like being the only non-Liverpudlian in Hamburg?*

Answer: It was scary - they all sounded so damn dangerous - more so than, say, a Cockney - but less so than a Glaswegian from the Gorbals. (By contrast, a Norwich/Norfolk accent "strokes the senses"!). When a Scouser said to: - "Piss Off!" (even when it was meant affectionately) there was nothing endearing about it - at least to my (Norwich) ears. (At the CNS - our school - they couldn't have spoken that uncouthly...). They sounded hard - but I <u>looked</u> it!

Comment: *Pictures of TS from that time would validate this: he did have quite an aggressive facade back in his Norfolk days. Indeed he had so much pent-up energy back then that one would be forgiven for thinking he had a dose of *St. Vitus's dance. And then there's the story of his marathon fist fight with Pete Best - Tony wasn't always the gentle guy he is now.*

Footnote: Named after St Vitus the third century patron saint and another name for the rather archaic medical condition Sydenham's chorea - to the layman an inability to control the limbs. Musically Elvis Presley probably had it even before Tony!

Question: *It's been suggested Gene Vincent sang "My Bonnie" on stage - I know he didn't record it. (I am familiar with the Ray Charles version).*

Answer: Knowing Gene's version (having backed Gene on many occasions) gave me the impetus to do it "properly" with the Beatles. Ray's version was, as always, untouchable and above criticism.

Comment: *It's been clear whilst interviewing Tony that he rates Ray Charles almost above any other modern day artiste. But re Tony's answer, the author was surprised to hear that Gene used to sing "My Bonnie". It's not listed in the very full discography of Vincent's output by Derek Henderson, which even includes Gene's known live recordings. But, as they say, Tony was there so he should know.*

It's a brief digression but I remember Tony telling me that Ray Charles had listened to the former doing his spot on the Star Club bill and would remark to someone who was standing nearby, "That cat's got soul!" Frustratingly for Tony this compliment was only passed on to him much later and as something of an afterthought! A huge Ray Charles fan, there's a brief entry on Ray in the Glossary, it's a remark Tony has deeply cherished ever since.

Question: *You knew Horst Fascher? He was about in 1992 - is he still? (Fascher was originally a bouncer on the doors at the Kaiserkeller club in Hamburg when he met both The Beatles and TS.)*

Answer: What can one say about Horst Fascher? To be sure, there is much that could be said - but it would open up too many old wounds, and I'm not about to do a character study of the man. In fact, it would serve no purpose to do so. To do him justice: he was, in some ways, not inconsequential in his role as "musicians' watchdog" in the period 1960 - 1967. His presence was either benign or outright dangerous - depending on your loyalties.

Comment: *Horst went with Tony to Vietnam and there's much more about him later when we arrive at Tony's Vietnam sojourn. There's also a Glossary entry under his name.*

Question: *I recently bought a Polydor double CD release, The Beatles' featuring Tony Sheridan, with all those Hamburg recordings in both mono and stereo. Do you get monies for these or were you ripped off somewhat like Lonnie Donegan and his miserly session fee for "Rock Island Line"? (I also mentioned I thought Tony had taken action re royalties in the U.S. courts. Not unusual given there's a showbiz maxim 'Where there's a Hit, there's a Writ').*

Answer: I'm working on it. Victory still eludes me, but I'm working on it. Lonnie really got ripped off. Can't relate to the mention of "U.S. courts". However, in Germany it may well come to that, depending on who tires earlier. Again, I'm workin' on it.

Comment: *It may not have paid the rent of course but TS did eventually get awarded a Gold Disc for his recording of "My Bonnie" when he was backed by the Beatles. A replica of it hangs in his Hamburg home.*

Question: *George Harrison did say about you that there were some (quote) hire purchase problems. Hellishly historic but does this mean something to you? I added in capitals, at this point, Don't let any questions offend you - if necessary hide behind the Fifth Amendment!*

Answer No.1: Oh, a trivial matter which I had to sort out. One wasn't a Saint.

Comment: *To clarify, this concerned an H.P. agreement, for a guitar, signed in England before he went over to Germany. But Tony is being far too disingenuous regarding this episode which even made the Norwich papers from memory. I eventually managed to wheedle quite a bit more about this episode out of him, as is now revealed in answer number 2 below.*

Answer No.2: In those days if one wasn't yet 21, a "guarantor" had to be found. The one I found was a character called Reg Calvert, a music manager not especially popular with some young musicians, e.g. with myself. Everything was fine until I went to Hamburg and "forgot" to pay the instalments! However, I went back to "face the music" and clear things up. As I showed sufficient contrition, and ventured back voluntarily the magistrate let me off, saying pay £20 to the Red Cross and don't be naughty again. I have not been naughty since.

Back in London horrendous tales of very naughty musicians had been circulating for some time, the "art" required that one didn't get caught. Had I stayed in the U.K., and kept up with the instalments nothing would've come of it. But performing in Hamburg-St. Pauli was akin to playing on another planet, and London seemed so far away!

Comment: *But there is even more to this "trivial matter" and a full confessional in Tony's own words would eventually follow and is included here to finally put this episode to bed.*

Answer No.3: As you know during 1960 I was having a lot of success so I was very surprised indeed when the German police arrived on my doorstep one day and insisted that I had to resolve this outstanding hire purchase thing by returning home. Of course if I'd remained playing in Britain at the time and not been in Hamburg this problem would never have arisen anyway as the hire purchase payments would almost certainly have been made, but once I'd moved abroad it wasn't anywhere near as straight forward or easy to do. But anyway I straightaway voluntarily agreed to return to England to get the matter resolved once and for all. But it began to get heavy from the start when I was met by two plain clothes detectives back in London and escorted to the West End Central Police Station where I had to stay locked up overnight.

It came as quite a surprise I can tell you as so many musicians back then had bought guitars in exactly the same way as I had with, perhaps, little thought for the consequences. In fact I then ended up being remanded with another musician Buddy Britten, who along with his manager Reg Calvert, was also due to be dealt with by the local magistrates. I was duly brought before a judge but rather than deal with the matter he remanded me for 10 days which I had to spend in Brixton Prison surrounded by hardened criminals. I was put in 'solitary' and in the long days that followed was made to scrub floors whilst of course I wasn't permitted cigarettes. At the time the whole thing seemed incredibly tough in contrast to my life in Hamburg and I have to tell you that I prayed nightly for help to see me through. I was eventually brought back to court and given a finger-wagging by the magistrate who suggested I pay reparation by donating £50 (*author - any advance on £50?*) to the Red Cross. Obviously I had no alternative but to agree but then had to wait around again until I could get the money sent over from Germany. So there you have it Alan. It happened, but in retrospect it all seems a storm in a teacup and one can't see anything similar happening today. But everything happens for a reason and I have no regrets.

Comment: *Third time lucky and we have the full story, which certainly has the ring of truth. Incidentally the author remembers seeing Buddy Britten and the Regents on stage in Norwich during 1962 on a bill headed by Jerry Lee Lewis - it was his comeback tour - who was also supported by Johnny Kidd and the Pirates, Vince Eager and others. Buddy, as you might guess, was literally a Holly look-alike who never made the British charts and little would be seen of him thereafter. A guitar genius himself, Tony professes not to have rated the Holly-influenced guitar player's prowess very highly.*

Question: *What is your attitude to Germany/German people? I'm assuming you get good vibes.*

Answer: This is quite a question, entailing as it does answers which will vary much in content, depending on the period referred to. Obviously, "1944" will yield a far different - but still authentic - reply than say "1960" or "1993" or "2001". Contradictory attitudes will, naturally, emerge, and, in the process of a verbal conversation/interview, probably the entire "mess" will cathart (*Tony's understandably rusty English here produces a verb from the word "cathartic", but the meaning is clear*). Assuming the question is consciously posed … (*it was*) this could be the subject of a lengthy essay or even a book.

Where to begin? Firstly, <u>all</u> of my experiences with Germans and Germany (West and East) can be viewed essentially as encounters between two <u>foreigners</u>, viz them and me, (and on <u>their</u> ground!). Secondly, T. Sheridan being a professional musician, is not a typical "anything" or "anybody", but rather he is the member of a very small minority group known as "foreign musicians active in Germany". Thirdly, his early upbringing was, of necessity, heavily biased against nearly all things German or Teutonic except the teachings of Luther! Somehow the non-German world managed to de-Germanise German classical music by tacitly classing Brahms, Beethoven, Schubert, Handel, Haydn, Weber, etc., etc. as being agents of a higher inspirational order, more in league with God and his Angels, than a cultural aspect of a mere, geographically determined, earthly race of barbarians located in the North-West of Europe. My mother subscribed to this theory. (Pronouncing "Luther" as if it were an English word did much to soften the corners of this otherwise very German-sounding name!).

And, of course, Mozart (despite being Austrian) was in a class of his own, defying categorisation. (Although that reprobate fellow Wagner, snubbing his nose at God, managed to combine elements of Heaven and Hell in <u>his</u> compositions, Heaven usually subjugating Hell by the heavy persuasion of the Lord's Will.) But I have digressed too far from the topic…

My attitude towards Germany, Germans, and things German simply defies formulation of that/those attitude(s). At this time, I have simply no inclination to begin to describe an attitude I may or may not have. All nations have their quirks, as do all individuals. I'd rather not say anything about Germany that could be misconstrued to mean something else - hopefully this attitude doesn't prove harmful to, or offend, any of my German friends…

There is a simple explanation for my reticence. As Paul McCartney would in all likelihood concede, Germany presented us with the possibility of presenting us with the opportunity of developing our artistic leanings to the full. Without Hamburg, would we have developed the Beatles' music? My love and affection for the Germans certainly supersedes any holier-than-thou "winning-side" pretensions I may have had in my early youth.

Comment: *It would be pointless for the author to add to these very full comments.*

Question: *What about the fact that so many individuals have been spoken of as the Fifth Beatle? (Alternatively, an American writer in a lengthy 1994 profile would head his article, Tony Sheridan - The First Beatle).*

Answer: The Fifth Beatle is one of those misleading labels, coined by the press to confuse the public. But why the Beatles? Why not the "Fifth Rolling Stone" or the "Seventh Moody Blues". The absurdity of extending group membership to provide a subject for discussion, a hypothetical reality, might well include Aunt Mimi, Peter Sellers, Spike Milligan, or even the toilet-lady in the Top Ten club…But not, hopefully, Yoko Ono! (If Bob Dylan sees fit to invent himself or any other Bob Dylans in order to understand the world better, then that is his business, and his prerogative alone. That way he anticipates the media's crap, and neatly nips their gripes in the bud. The guy's a genius…). P.S. I rate myself as the best T.S. imitator/impersonator around - though strictly speaking, I am "only" a copy of a copy.

Comment: *Pointed comments re the Fifth Beatle, but with some humour thrown in. *George Best, *George Martin, even *Jimmy Tarbuck where did the list ever end? And perhaps briefly, in a recording studio in Hamburg, circa 1961... Tony Sheridan was indeed fleetingly the Fifth Beatle, even if he has no wish to stake a claim for such a spurious title.*

**Footnote:* The names above illustrate just how ridiculously varied are the individuals who've been put forward in the long list of possible fifth Beatles. One (George Best, 1946-2005) a late footballing genius from that same era, the next (Sir George Martin, born 1926) the legendary producer of The Beatles during their greatest years while the last named (Jimmy Tarbuck, born 1940) a fellow Scouser who appeared on stage with The Beatles in the '60s, most famously when they played a Royal Command Performance at the London Palladium.

Question: *You were used as part of an early Beatles video biography (The Compleat Beatles) but were you approached in the '90s re the major Beatles Anthology?*

Answer: Not re the book or the music.

Comment: *That must have been a disappointment. Once again, Tony became little more than a minor footnote. An oversight in the author's opinion although he claims to have been happy just to get a mention.*

Question: *The first time the Beatles actually saw Sheridan on stage was at the Studio X club. I asked him why they clicked so quickly?*

Answer: It was helped by the fact that they were more articulate than the average group of musicians and, in addition, we had the link of an art or grammar school background which helped too. They were interesting people and we would all pick up things from one another, and it didn't seem long before we were all dressed in leather and wearing cowboy boots!"

Comment: *But it was the Kaiserkeller - it was in a side street in the Grosse Freiheit - where TS and the Beatles would jam and he was asked for his opinion of the club.*

Answer: It was the pits!

Comment: *That's almost a shorter answer than the name, Kaiserkeller, which incidentally means Emperor's winery. It seems that when on stage their German promoter would shout "mach schau! mach schau!" both encouraging and irritating the British performers in equal measure. And although it seems a curious co-incidence that the German "mach schau" sounds phonetically like the command to "make show", i.e. put on a show, TS says a truer interpretation would actually be to "get with it!". He also remembers that back then the raucous audiences just wanted the singer to wiggle his legs as much as possible. This fact plus the way TS, The Beatles or others would improvise lyrics must have made for an interesting listening experience back then.*

...Tony himself would stay in Hamburg, with a residency at one club or another, for the next few years while The Beatles would find themselves forever shuttling back and forth between Germany and Britain, clocking up an incredible five Hamburg visits before their fame finally outgrew the scene there. Both groups of musicians, Sheridan and The Beatles, had started out at relatively small club venues, (Sheridan was at the Kaiserkeller, The Beatles at the Indra, which means India in German) but both would eventually play the biggest and best club in Hamburg the legendary, if short-lived Star-Club (The original club would open in 1960 and close two years later, but not before Jerry Lee Lewis had cut one the most famous rock and roll albums there, modestly entitled Greatest Live Show On Earth.) And famously, the Beatles would also be recorded live there in 1962 and a poor quality album, The Beatles Tapes, would eventually surface and make a brief UK chart appearance in 1976. Tony himself, when looking back, would have a tainted view of the Star-Club, *"it had become sordid and decadent. People only liked it because they could get to see Jerry Lee Lewis for a *couple of Deutsch Marks."*

Footnote: Literally a few pounds sterling.

So just what <u>did</u> he achieve in those four or five years (1963/1967), between the lengthy plateau of his original arrival in Hamburg, which had peaked by '63, and the moment when he came to leave it all behind for Vietnam? Well he'd certainly become disillusioned with the way his life and career were heading by the time 1967 had rolled into view. It's not been too easy to reconstruct just what was going on day by day, even with Tony's help, but it's known that during the '60s he was at times shuttling back and forth to the U.K., either to back some touring American act, or else doing some solo gigs while billed as The Tony Sheridan Trio. Then we've heard how he'd approached Brian Epstein for help but had little that was tangible to show for his efforts by the time he arrived back in Germany.

However he still managed to stay busy with his label Polydor putting out a string of singles under his name which were reasonably successful, even if they didn't exactly storm the charts. As mentioned two made the German Top Ten charts, or the Hit Bilanz as it was called. Meanwhile, throughout 1964, those recordings that he'd made with The Beatles three years earlier, were now beginning to pepper the lower reaches of the U.S. charts and, although he wouldn't tour there at the time, he did undertake a tour of

Australia where his recording of "Why" (a self-composition) had become quite a big hit. But before moving on to the immediate post-Beatles era we need to have a look at that momentous Sheridan recording session which just happened to involve four soon-to-be-famous Liverpudlians…well three (sorry Pete).

CHAPTER 8: THE "MY BONNIE" SESSIONS OF JUNE 21st/23rd, 1961

"Now I'm Older and I Can See
They All Meant the Best For Me
But They Don't Know There's Nothing Else
Than I Would Rather Be
Than a Rock 'n' Roll Player In a Hard-Rock Band"

When I Was Young Composer - Tony Sheridan

INTRODUCTION:

Despite all that's been said about Sheridan's musical life thus far it's a believe-it-or-not fact that he's never really broken sweat trying to get into mainstream pop at all, as deep down it just isn't his bag. He wasn't the first and won't be the last to hitch a ride on whatever music was in vogue as a means to an end: and the end in Tony's case certainly wasn't pop music per se. Indeed whenever a discussion on music comes up he is apt to disparage mainstream pop insisting music is all about the content, or as he puts it: *"it's the feel, the groove, the tempo that's important."* Despite these strong, if suppressed feelings way back then, he was (for example) more than able to compose a decent ballad for the session, "Why (Don't You Love Again)", which was pure pop both in style and substance. In mitigation it includes a well-above-average number of Sheridan chord changes! But it also has some early Beatles harmonies on it for good measure.

So let's look at each of the songs in turn and there's really no need to employ a question and answer technique. Instead we'll purely list each song title recorded during those June, 1961 sessions followed by Tony's brief thoughts on each song in question. As some of his thoughts were rather general in nature and applied to the session as a whole, certain quotes have been tacked on at the end, together with the question as to why his backing group were labelled The Beat Brothers, rather than The Beatles. The recordings would first appear on the Polydor label, which is probably the best known German pop label having first been formed in 1924. During the '60s and '70s they had quite a bit of pop success, although for middle-of-the-road music lovers the label probably remains best known for the twin recordings of bandleaders Bert Kaempfert ("Wonderland by Night" was a gold record) and his best-selling compatriot, James Last. But rather than discuss the history of the record label let's turn to the music:

"Ain't She Sweet" (This was the only song title, apart from "Cry For a Shadow", an instrumental, where Sheridan didn't perform the lead vocals, which were taken by John Lennon.)

Tony: *"John's voice was bad at that time, as it was very overworked just then. On the other numbers he was happy to mostly stay out of it and back me."*

Note: Tony was present when the above number was recorded but didn't play on it. It belatedly reached No.19 in the US Billboard charts during 1964.

"Cry For a Shadow" (This was the only instrumental number, and it featured George Harrison on a self-composed - with John - number. Again Tony wasn't on it.)

Tony: *"I said George, you've got to do one. So this was George getting his chance and, by the way, he never did anything quite like that again."*

Note: As mentioned Tony had insisted George do an instrumental number which was of course George's tongue-in-cheek homage to The Shadows and similar to their current UK hit of the time, "The Frightened City". (So there were to be solos from both John and from George but, although not significant, nothing from Paul..)

"If You Love Me Baby" Tony Sheridan lead vocals, backed by John, Paul, George and Pete Best. This number is almost a duet between Tony and Paul on bass.

Tony: *"I had heard Jimmy Reed, the blues man, do it but Elvis was a strong influence on me then, so I decided to do it like Elvis. It's a simple song, a blues, and as we needed songs for the session I learnt it and did it the next day. But it is the worst guitar solo I ever did in my life!"*

Note: Meeting up with McCartney many years later Paul recalled their collaboration on this number with particular affection: after all he was the new boy on bass at the time and was relieved that the recording worked so well, despite Tony's dissatisfaction with his own guitar playing.

"My Bonnie" Again Tony lead vocals, backed by the four Beatles, playing and doing the Duane Eddy inspired rebel yells! Of course this was the big record from the session, inasmuch as TS would get eventually get a Gold Record for it.

Tony: *"The song wasn't usually in my repertoire so it was a freak thing really. Although it was a joke you can still do a joke well! But look, I also did it because the German public would have known the song from their own childhoods".*

Note: It's ironic that the best known number from the session (it was also a big hit on the continent) was included as an afterthought, almost as a joke. And, incidentally it's the only number from the session that featured some of the song sung in German. (There were to be an English language 'introduction' version and an alternative German 'introduction' version recorded - no doubt Beatles fans will have both. They were both included on the double CD Polydor release of a few years back)

"Nobody's Child" It's the same line-up on this and the remaining tracks.

Tony: *"I got into it because I'd had an unhappy childhood. Lonnie's version was more folk and I tried not to copy it and instead put a bit of Elvis into it. I do the song to this day - and the emotion still comes out."*

Note: It's a song which takes Tony back to his skiffle roots. "Nobody's Child" is a plaintive number he'd fallen in love with on first listening to Lonnie Donegan's 1956 Showcase album and, even if he didn't consciously register the fact, the lyrics expressed and encompassed the rejection he'd always felt in his personal life. George would do the number as a Travelling Wilbury years later.

"The Saints" The same line-up as above. The song is the traditional standard often given its longer title "When the Saints Go Marching In" e.g. as per Bill Haley, and earlier jazz groups.

Tony:*"I'd been listening to Jerry Lee Lewis a lot and his rendition of 'Old Black Joe' in particular. I was also a fan of Chris Barber and of course all jazz bands did The Saints, as it was commonly known. There are only a couple of chords in it and you're* *able to do it in your own way. Mine owes quite a lot to Jerry Lee!"*

Note: No need to remind readers that The Saints also just happened to be the name of Tony's original group back in Norfolk. Of course, for every jazz and skiffle fan back then, this was a staple number and one that Tony had been brought up on, so it was relatively obvious choice for him to make.

"Sweet Georgia Brown" Again, same line up - the number had been popular for years having been written back in 1925.

Tony: *"We were trying to be different. It was a catchy number but we felt it hadn't been done before in a rock 'n' roll vein."*

Note: Tony felt the number lent itself well to being rocked up. He remembers that he would tackle the number many times but the first time in the studio was with The Beatles doing instrumental and vocal backings.

"Why (Can't You Love Me Again)" Same line up - finally doing a Sheridan song - with the Beatles employing some good harmonies in the background.

Tony: *"I just needed to write a song about love, so I wrote a ballad and there are actually six or seven chords in it".*

Note: Although William Crompton, Tony's booking agent for a time, is listed as co-writer, TS insists the song was all his own work. Certainly the lyrics echo aspects of Tony's own life even if he wasn't in the least conscious of that at the time he penned it.

Postscript: It can be seen (above) that the author has stuck to the basic known recordings made with The Beatles as discussed with Tony, but it is a veritable mine-field when trying to discover exactly who sang on what and when and where etc. A recent learned book on that whole Hamburg period (1960 to 1962) eloquently made the point that there has been a great deal of conflicting talk over the years on that subject and it is not the author's intention to fuel the flames. Thus, the present work does not claim to be authoritative but rather seeks to illuminate Tony's life which has been badly overlooked when discussing the history of 1960s pop music up to now. In throwing fresh light on his story hopefully readers will have been persuaded to seek out his later recordings. There's a great deal to enjoy.

And now for a few more Sheridan thoughts on those sessions:

With hindsight he's certainly annoyed that the numbers they recorded were such a hotchpotch, and weren't even representative of what they were playing nightly on stage. Here's how Tony remembers Bert Kaempfert explaining it, *"Come into the studio, play some tracks and I will put it to Polydor. At the start there was no guarantee that an album would be released. Moreover he felt we should look for Public Domain material so Polydor could get themselves part of any income. That was the way it was at that time."* As to what material to choose Tony says, *"we were able to play any number of titles from our combined repertoire effortlessly. It's regrettable that so few typical songs emerged - hardly one title containing a single weird chord worthy of the name!"* And a chance was missed, or as he puts it: *"it should surely have occurred to someone - but it didn't - to record an evening's live performance. What a shame..."*

He also remembers how he took charge during the studio sessions back then,

"Look, I directed John or Paul to play this or whatever was needed and said, then I'll play such and such, although bear in mind that I always improvised and would never ever play something the same way twice." In giving his take on the sessions he expands on this thinking: *"I just wanted to get on a record and this was my chance. The Beatles thought the same but this wasn't their chance - that would come later".* So let's spell it out for what it was: in recording Tony Sheridan, Bert Kaempfert was giving the singer a huge break, and The Beatles were only incidental to the main plot. Tony puts it yet another way when saying with total candour: *"look, we would have paid him to make a record! We were very excited, it was a big deal. And if it had to be done this way, that was fine."*

That thought really says it all: these were simply one-off sessions, put together by the Polydor maestro at short notice and pretty cheaply too. Of course they were fairly successful although, in hindsight, Tony remains surprised that Kaempfert didn't spot the obvious potential of John, Paul and George. *"How short-sighted can you get in not recognising the talent of The Beatles?"* This has been said many times over the years and no doubt it was a thought that was to exercise Kaempfert's own mind too for several years thereafter.

Asked for the hundredth time why he called his backing group The Beat Brothers rather than The Beatles or anything else, Tony gave what was probably his standard response: *"When the Beatles played in Hamburg they were always called The Beatles. They weren't the Silver Beatles or any other kind of Beatles, but they were known as The Beat Brothers for recording purposes. This came about because the record company (Polydor) thought that the name Beatles was silly, or even offensive especially for Germany, so I had to come up with a name that was acceptable to the German public. I then came up with The Beat Brothers, and they were very very good. They had a rhythm and blues style and it was very aggressive and very authentic but* (and here he's on controversial ground, but it's just Tony being Tony) *it wasn't pop music!"*

And that, believe it or not, is actually said as a compliment given that so much general pop music back then was decidedly bland. Later he admits to feeling more than a bit disappointed when he first heard the group's recording of "Love Me Do" wondering if they'd sold out by making what appeared to him to be a second rate pop record. But, he quickly adds, *"that was only until I heard their more inventive stuff, when I was to quickly revise my opinion!"*

And an Afterword

There has been a great deal of conflicting talk over the years about which studio recordings The Beatles definitely played on back in Hamburg (particularly "Swanee River") before their climb to fame. The author has checked with both the 1997 Hans Olof Gottfridsson book, The Beatles - From Cavern to Star-Club a 470 page tome, as well as a later book by the French Beatles expert Eric Krasker, The Beatles: Fact and Fiction: 1960-1962, but quickly realised that it would be foolish to cross swords with genuine Beatles experts. Instead I opted to look briefly at each song title and ask Tony for some random thoughts. Anyone wishing to delve deeper further can readily do so - perhaps a first step being to consult both the books mentioned above (see Bibliography).

The basic facts remain that the recordings were made over a three day period in June of 1961 with TS and The Beatles both having signed separate contracts with Polydor the month before under the auspices of the German bandleader and main man, Bert Kaempfert. The adapted studio where the sessions took place was in fact unlike the conventional recording studio but was actually an orchestra hall situated within an infants school, known as the Harburg Friedrich Ebert Halle and situated quite close to Hamburg. Evidently portable equipment would be brought in by the record company which was capable of making state of the art stereo masters on site and, according to the engineer from those days, Karl Hinze, the premises had superb acoustics and those recordings still sound good today.

Other later Hamburg recordings by Sheridan circa 1961-1962 would find him backed by a mixture of musicians from The Big Six, The Star Combo or others, but regardless of who actually played, all in effect were termed Beat Brothers. As implied the description wasn't intended to be significant as the same musicians invariably played in one or more of the outfits and were mostly gigging with TS on a nightly basis. Despite his plethora of German releases the only records which cracked the Top 10 there during this time were "Skinny Minnie" and the dance number "Let's Slop". Surprisingly "My Bonnie" was only a minor hit stalling at No. 32 nationally although it did reach the Top 10 in a Hamburg Hit List of the day. One researcher on Sheridan's early German recordings indicates that around 27 recordings (that's inclusive of the "My Bonnie" sessions) were made over a two year period. As an interesting postscript, TS would return to the same Hamburg studio in 2007 and create some more recordings with a group of young musicians from Tanzania. The troubadour returns…

CHAPTER 9: HAMBURG : THE POST-BEATLES PERIOD

"I'm moving on - a lotta things in life are wrong
Now all I want to say:
That it really was a dismal day"

Maine and Back Again. Composer - Tony Sheridan

BACK-STORY: As the 1960s progressed, the German rock 'n' roll scene lost whatever impetus it briefly had, and we will shortly be led onwards to a war-torn Vietnam where he and his group entertained the troops before being awarded honorary decorations by the U.S. Army: presumably for entertaining, perhaps for just surviving! Unsettled by all he had seen he would then become engrossed in the whole transcendental scene although, it must be noted, not as part of the famous Maharishi/Beatles caravan but via his own individual path. Instead Tony, still then outwardly aggressive if inwardly fragile, was determined to seek out a meaning and purpose in life even if it compromised or derailed his musical career. He did actually dip his toe in the emerging transcendental meditation scene in Germany but then changed direction to become a devoted follower of another guru, the Bhagwan Shree Rajneesh (1931-1990), a hugely influential Indian spiritual teacher of the day. Indeed the name still resonates as the founder of the worldwide Osho movement, an organisation that is still in existence years after the Bhagwan's own passing. Tony insists that this was right for him at the time and indeed the Bhagwan's teachings have stayed with him and still guide him to this day. There's much more to come on this fascinating topic - and as I was to discover it's not a frivolous topic either - it's one that remains a central pillar of his life.

Question: *Your biographical details list you as in Germany from 1960-67. Can you flesh that period out a bit more?*

Answer: Regarding 1960-67 I resided mostly in Germany. Arriving in Hamburg - St. Pauli in June '60 meant a permanent break with the past on all levels - our (the "Jets" and I) arrival was the equivalent of a "planet change" after which nothing resembled the past that we had just left behind …except the music. Music was the anchor, and the ship in which we were - collectively speaking - still at home ("the same boat"…); and music was sanity, the proverbial straw on which to cling, a way of life, one's very substance. Without music life would be unimaginably empty and devoid of meaning. If Soho had been the frying-pan, then St. Pauli meant a gigantic leap into the fire. "Fire" implies, life, emotion, zeal, heat, inspiration, excitement, fever and …light. Although light also suggests shadow - and St. Pauli had lots of that . How could it be otherwise in one square kilometre of assorted abominations?

One could muse - and rightly - that our coming brought a good amount of sustenance to a starving community. By this I allude to the music and all it entailed - and what it would mean to future generations, not only in Hamburg. The ramifications of the ensuing music scene subsequently lead to essential fundamental changes - not only in Germany - but in the whole of continental Europe, Great Britain, and ultimately over the big pond, where the Beatles and others challenged the very foundations of rock music. Even the "all-knowing" Bob Dylan thought it safe to say that British bands "cannot play rock 'n' roll" - but sooner than later he abandoned this conceit for a safer philosophy which allowed for Elvis', Chuck Berry's, Buddy Holly's, Little Richard's influence to have taken root and blossomed in London, Newcastle, Sheffield, Glasgow and Dublin - and yes, at a tangent, also in that most unlikely of places: Hamburg's St. Pauli district.

Oh, Alan, let's not forget fine Norwich City, which, in several roundabout ways, has not a little influence on the growth of rock music! In Hamburg, throughout the period 1960-67, music was continually re-birthing itself, the curve of its parabolic progression finally sinking into oblivion in the late '60s, never to assert itself again. But the real raison d'etre of Hamburg's music scene had fulfilled its purpose in providing a campus for the willing-to-learn musical fraternity, and this in a most collaborative fashion.

Earnest players and performers found a ready-made forum that sported several arenas, just waiting for the contestants to mount the stage. At the height of the scene, it was awesome for young musicians - mostly from Britain - to find themselves performing on the same boards which, only last week, were weighted by Ray Charles' 18 piece orchestra, and the week before by Jerry Lee Lewis with a band from the U.K. (Chas from Chas and Dave - see Glossary under Chas Hodges.) One could quite easily be featured on the same bill as Fats Domino or Bo Diddley. (Of course, after Jerry Lee's stint, the piano on the Star Club stage had to be repaired and tuned in time for Ray Charles' performance.)

Looking back, I have a strong suspicion that Hamburg was an inevitability, predestined by "destiny" to provide seven years of "training opportunity" for young performers who otherwise would not have found a comparable chance anywhere else. Certainly, a comparable scene did not exist - not in the U.S. nor in North West Europe or Scandinavia - at that time. Personally I have to subscribe to the somewhat "potty" view, viz. that a sort of divine providence was at work, bringing certain characters together, at "the right time, in the right place", in order to produce a certain result the long-term effects of which would ultimately benefit mankind.

As I have said before, one obvious and indisputable early result was reconciliation - of an unusual kind, admittedly. That rock 'n' roll music could bring young people together - whose parents had only recently been at each other's throats - in the throes of World War Two is, to my mind, nothing short of amazing. But that is precisely what happened. Tony Blair (*Prime Minister at the time of Tony's quote*) would, I'm sure, endorse this view. Had he been PM back then, he might even have had the foresight to instigate such an action in the interest of Anglo-German relations. After all, he had had aspirations in the rock 'n' roll world!

Comment: *Certain seemingly routine questioning would occasionally, spur Tony to the most lengthy and introspective of musings. It's certainly not rambling, as it's the author's opinion that he held pretty consistent views throughout our collaboration. Incidentally, Tony would either back, or appear on the same Star Club bill in those days as Tommy Roe, Brenda Lee, Emile Ford, Johnny Kidd and several others in addition to the acts he mentioned above. A whole lot of acts appeared on that stage in a relatively brief time-frame.*

Question: *How many times married, number of children/grandchildren etc? (Not sure if this is a sensitive area given your own upbringing).*

Answer: My present marriage is not the first, and I have several children - great and small. Most of them are 50% German, 50% their Dad, and 100% European and "anti-border". (Borders are dangerous things - most wars are started because of them. As a famous teacher once remarked, an astronaut, when viewing our planet from space, has not yet discovered a single national border. A natural boundary is something entirely different - it has its advantages as well as its drawbacks. Fortunately, modern travel now overcomes many of the drawbacks...).

Comment: *In my adult life I have spent a considerable time in Tony's company yet he has always put up a wall of silence when asked about his private life, although back in 2010 he did mention in passing that apart from his children he had two grandchildren from his first marriage. In many ways he's truly saddened by the way things have turned out saying at one point, "I was always looking for a long term relationship and never for anything tawdry."*

Question: *I read a review of you backing Gene Vincent at The Speakeasy in London circa 1969 with Georgie Fame also backing. Memories? (I got this from the Sweet Gene Vincent book by Steven Mandich - see Bibliography).*

Answer: Do not recall ever having accompanied Gene in the "Speakeasy". Certainly not with Georgie Fame. If *Laurie O'Leary knew your face and liked you, you stood a good chance of getting in. Went down the drain (the club) when it got too "posh" for the punters. You could meet any number of faces down there. For many years it was the "in" place for the Soho/West End scene, more especially for the musicians.

**Footnote:* A legendary London show-biz figure who was in artiste management as well as a tour manager to many. Has also written a seminal biography of Ronnie Kray, one of the notorious Kray Twins.

Comment: *The Gene Vincent book clearly lists Tony and Georgie Fame as 'guesting' on a gig but as it was a one-off and almost 40 years on it's perhaps not surprising he can't recall this particular night. (As the reader may have guessed the author is a huge Vincent fan so any opportunity to question Tony on the rock 'n' roll legend has been taken!).*

Question: *Lived in Oregon, USA when? Why? This is part of trying to establish some sort of chronology.*

Answer: Back in the early eighties, I wanted very much to move to Oregon permanently. Bhagwan had founded a commune there on what was earlier known as the "Big Muddy Ranch", a relic of John Wayne western epics. The land itself has been reduced to a desert - biologically dead, except for the juniper population - by excessive cattle grazing followed by sheep-farming and too little irrigation. The (mostly American) commune residents managed to transform the "ranch" into a veritable garden. Unfortunately, U.S. immigration decided (under Reagan) not to issue permanent residence permits to visitors from elsewhere. However, on festival occasions, upwards of 10,000 visitors were recorded during the "highlight" periods.

Consider for a minute - *Cat Stevens wouldn't receive even a visitor's permit for the U.S.!!! And if he wasn't British, Tony Blair wouldn't let him in either!!! I get upset about some things, I really do. Consider also: if Jesus came back and went to America, they'd crucify him on the White House lawn... Sometimes I almost despair - but not for long. After all, it's only a game isn't it?

**Footnote:* Cat Stevens (born in London, 1947 as Steven Georgiou) had a huge run of UK hits spanning the '60s and '70s before suddenly quitting the music business and converting to the Islamic faith while adopting the name of Yusuf Islam. It seemed at one time that he had totally forsaken music but he returned to the recording studio in the 1990s albeit sporting his Islamic identity. These days he is also known as an active humanitarian and philanthropist.

Comment: *Tony remains a devout follower of the teachings of the late Bhagwan Shree Rajneesh, taking the name, Swami Prabha Sharan, which the author was told literally means "At the feet of God". It is a thought that Tony daily tries to keep at the forefront of his mind. There's a bit more about the Bhagwan, and his philosophy, in the Glossary section.*

Question: *What about the Maharishi Mahesh Yogi who the Beatles studied under in the late '60s? Guess you were in Vietnam at that time?*

Answer: As a teacher, he offered learnable meditation techniques at a reasonable price. Established religion left him alone, apparently seeing in his person neither threat to the church itself nor to its teachings. At any rate, at a time in my life when I was more "down than up", it seemed like a good idea to get myself a mantra. From various acquaintances I had heard of the benefits of Transcendental Meditation, although I was not especially drawn towards the Maharishi's philosophy or person. So armed with a fresh white handkerchief, some fresh fruit and flowers, I went along to the local T.M. centre to receive "my" mantra. One is told by the instructor that the mantra (in my case a Sanskrit-sounding word of two syllables) is tailored to one's personal requirements and personality traits…(Well, it worked fine, in that I relaxed - meditatively speaking - for two 20 minute sessions a day, and gradually began to discard some of my heavy "body armour" for a calmer, more optimistic, outlook, which in turn entailed opening one's eyes to one's hang-ups and quirks.) In short, becoming altogether a more positive human being. When I went back to the centre 2-3 weeks later for a "check-up" the instructor was amazed at the obvious change for the better. The benefits were indisputable - the drawbacks nil. Whatever the Beatles thought of him as a person/teacher, his technique worked. (If a physician lusts after someone's female friend, it does not mean that he is not a good doctor!) Whatever - "Sexy Sadie" and other negative publicity left Maharishi unscathed but smarting.

Comment: *I like the opening thought that teachings were available "at a reasonable price." And reference the last few sentences - Beatles fans will doubtless appreciate that allusion.)*

Question: *What about the book When the Shoe Fits by the Bhagwan that you were continually reading when you first stayed at my house in 1986.*

Answer: Osho (Bhagwan) was the light-bringer for me and countless others. One of the truly great hopes for humanity. Murdered by Ronald Reagan and his cronies…

Comment: *Tony's involvement with the Bhagwan was total and much more follows later on this cherished aspect of his life.*

It can be seen that the years under review were anything but idle ones but equally there was little cohesive pattern or structure to them either. Apart from the approach he made to Epstein he had also chatted with Mickie Most and Henry Henroid (who have separate Glossary entries) back in England, both of whom Tony knew from their Soho days together, and it was even proposed that he should join a new label and a lively new song entitled, "Puppet On a String" would be his opening release! Now most may know that the number eventually became a huge hit for someone else and ended up as part of *Eurovision Song Contest folklore, but the suggestion that Tony record it was given short shrift by him - although for reasons that he can't really remember now. Maybe it just lacked appeal: certainly the lyrics suited a female singer better and Sandie Shaw duly made it into a UK No.1. Whatever the reasons, it seems Tony was developing into an individual who either just couldn't or wouldn't be helped. Life could soon swing out of kilter and he was feeling increasingly dissatisfied and a quote in the musical press from those days has him sounding increasingly exasperated: *"I got out of showbiz in 1967, and I've been floating around doing what I like, rather than being used by the record companies"*. But surely there was more to it than that trite comment? On the surface maybe not, but there was quite a lot going on at a sub-conscious level in the Sheridan mind that's for sure…

Footnote: The long-running annual music contest that has changed a lot over the years and these days even includes countries such as Israel - hardly a European country by any stretch of the imagination. Whilst Britain often won it in the early years (the '50s and '60s) these days the contest is far more partisan and the British entries are sadly more often than not also-rans.

CHAPTER 10: VIETNAM

"On the way it was tough, seen more shit than enough
There were mornings when the sun would not rise,
Through a dim Arcadian screen flashed a steel amber green,
Reflecting in the animal eyes"

*This Time***.** Composer - Tony Sheridan

BACK-STORY: So why was Tony the musician unable, incapable or seemingly unwilling to cash in on the domestic German success that had come his way? Well, for a start, he's always tended to have one toe dipped in the music business as a commercial venture while the rest of him has been well and truly anchored outside of it and, as a result, he's probably shunned any real fame and fortune. Instead following his heart rather than his head has been a lifelong weakness, but he himself has always felt that life was a journey to be savoured however many setbacks and heartaches might be encountered along the way. He said as much when reflecting on his actions about leaving Britain in 1960: *"Fate had stepped in. I went to Hamburg while following a hunch - a gut feeling."* Of course with so much happening in the outside world, and knowing Tony, there was little chance that he would ever opt for a conventional life-style and once again the wanderlust would take over his life. To some extent he would later rationalise his decision to move on by once again saying, *"I left again in 1967 as I knew that for me Hamburg was dead."* His private life was now increasingly unsettled and his musical career had become marooned in churning out the pop music of the day. But soon he'd be taking on a new challenge and getting into a totally different field of action, as by now he had made the radical decision to go to Vietnam and idealistically do his little bit for Freedom - with a capital F.

Although most readers will have heard of the Vietnam conflict a few sentences are needed to describe the backdrop, which was in reality a battle between two contrasting ideologies. The country of Vietnam, a former part of the French Union from the late 1940s, had begun to simmer away as a trouble spot in the 1950s and, despite the problems appearing to be an internal one between the military wings of the communist North and the non-communist South, the onset of the modern Vietnam era could be traced back to 1959 when two American advisers were killed in battle there. President Kennedy was on the point of taking over in the White House and it would become increasingly obvious that a conflict was brewing that would be destined to move centre stage and involve other world powers. The flashpoint that was Vietnam was to dominate politics well into the '70s and the years of major American involvement, generally given as 1965 through 1973, would see more than three million U.S. troops being involved overall at a cost to American tax-payers of over $120 billion, a fantastic cost back then. A massive number of American troops, close to 60,000, would eventually die in the jungles and rice fields of Vietnam and yet, towards the tail end of the '60s, we find Tony and some intrepid friends leaving the relatively safe shores of post-war West Germany for a life close to the front line, living among those self-same fighting forces…

Important Note re the remaining Chapters: We'll continue to use Tony's direct quotes whenever and wherever possible. It's worth pointing out that most of the initial quotes below had to be dragged out of him by the author: as earlier he'd covered that Far

Eastern period by brusquely saying, *"I'd been playing in Vietnam off and on from 1967 to 1970"*. But pressed, he would finally admit that life had been tough back then, and seated with the author in Tony's garden in Seestermuhe, near Hamburg (in May, 2007) he'd finally open up in reply to my promptings, with me busily jotting down his story in my own quaint shorthand while trying to keep up with his thought processes. So, given these circumstances it would be unfair to try and claim everything which follows to be direct quotes although it can be clearly seen where actual quotations are used, in contrast to when the story switches to an 'as told to' format. And, by the way, TS has always maintained that the narrative from his Vietnamese days would make the basis for an exciting film script. Personally I feel a *Warren Zevon song lyric might be closer, and "Roland the Headless Thompson Gunner" is the one that springs to mind! So let's start with some earlier quotes.

**Footnote:* The late US singer-songwriter Warren Zevon (1947-2003) is most famous for the extraordinarily sardonic lyrics that pepper his work. Check out such song-titles as Roland above, while "Werewolves of London" and "I'll Sleep When I'm Dead" run that pretty close.

Question: *You arrived in Vietnam around 1967, and you were there during a time when the conflict was escalating weren't you?*

Answer: Yes, when we arrived in Vietnam the US dead was 12,000, and when we left the figure had risen to 40,000.

Comment: *He did two 'tours' in Vietnam. The break in the middle would find him in Australia for a few months and that period will be covered shortly.*

Follow up point: *Initially Tony was idealistic about the Vietnam War and the words (the highly interesting words) below are taken from a letter to his mother, shortly after he arrived there:* "…I must tell you that this dirty business is a necessary factor in preventing a third world war involving the Red Chinese… Communism is evil for obvious reasons, and the only way to deal with it effectively in this case, when it threatens to spread and force people to bend under its rule, is to fight it…The Americans are on the side of good as opposed to evil, and there is no in between…"

Comment: *Powerful if extremely idealistic words from a man who was still in his 20s at this point but it was a view that would alter radically as the years went by and he increasingly began to realise that the moral high-ground wasn't just the preserve of any one ideology. He would sum up that time many years later by saying with some emotion, "the whole thing in Vietnam was just such a mess."*

Question: *But did he feel that he had enough songs, or the material necessary to entertain American troops?*

Answer: Yes, by now I had almost 200 songs in my repertoire and not only that but soul music was coming in at that time and I liked and sang soul too.

Comment: *So he was probably much better equipped than most to entertain such audiences given his love of soul. I also remember him giving me a more literal reason why he and his fellow musicians were chosen: it was simply to "employ some round-eyes musicians and entertainers" who would then remind the troops of home, rather than of* *the indigenous Vietcong!*

Question: *I think you came across drugs when you were there. Was it bad?*
Answer: The scene was far worse than what I'd experienced in Hamburg and drugs, with the connivance of the medics over there, were actually endemic throughout the military.
Comment: *Evidently it was much worse in the combat areas - although this was probably to be expected.*

Question: *(TS admits that the Americans had recruited his group and other entertainers in the first place to raise morale and take soldiers minds off the daily horror of war, however briefly.) I asked: did it affect you, what you were seeing?*
Answer: Look, I was screaming out my soul! I was singing out my soul for an audience that understood! If you sing from the soul it's enough to touch people and as for me, it was wonderful to be understood and looked up to. I would also get to sing 'White Christmas' or a gospel song like 'It Is No Secret (What God Can Do)' and the audience would be in tears.
Comment: *One of Tony's most poignant answers at this point and I noticed when discussing that whole period he could quickly become exceedingly passionate.*

Question: *So it's all still with you?*
Answer: Yes, my mind became badly messed up with the stress and strain of everything that happened to me back then. And it didn't disappear overnight either and I was really suffering badly for several years after it was all over. I still get traumatised to this day by any sudden explosions or even hearing fireworks going off can bring about flashbacks that I need to deal with.
Comment: *None needed.*

Question: *Tell me about the musicians that joined you for this tour of Vietnam? (The questions and his replies are taken from the notes I made when staying with Tony and Anna in early 2006).*
Reply (as told to the author/from notes made) : They weren't known stars, that's for sure, but were rather a select bunch of hand-picked volunteers from amongst the Hamburg scene. But they were a talented and tightly knit group who, spearheaded by Tony, had confidence in their own musical abilities to perform and entertain whenever and wherever they were needed, which was as near to the front line as was practical. There were four of them in all, although musically speaking the group were a multi-national threesome, plus one other, the manager and minder. The musical trio itself comprised the Shamrock-tinged-but-still-British-for-the moment leader, Tony, who performed vocals and doubled on guitar, while backing him would be a truly Irish drummer by the name of Jimmy Doyle, one of Tony's former Beat Brothers from Hamburg, with a competent German bassist by the name of Volker Tonndorf making up the group.

The remaining member of the party wasn't there just for the ride but was in fact Horst Fascher, the non-playing roadie and general factotum, and somebody whose name has briefly cropped up earlier. It should be said that Fascher was actually an infrequent singer so didn't really get involved very often on the musical front on this particular tour. When pressed to explain TS would confess that occasionally they'd cheerfully let him do one of his party pieces like "Be Bop a Lula" or "Hallelujah I Love Her So" (shades of karaoke) but mostly he left the music to the boys. As is known Horst was quite a hard man and his presence would lead to one or two hairy episodes as we'll hear shortly. (It seems that Horst was quite a character and TS would vividly describe him in these words, *"Look Alan, Horst Fascher was renowned as a popular thug in Hamburg. He mixed with the underworld all the time and was forever dealing in cards or in illegal gaming of some sort. And you must remember that Horst got on well with, and understood the black guys out there, so it was no surprise at all when things began to happen.")*

Technically the underlying engagement to entertain the troops there originally started out as a minimum of two weeks only, but an open-ended revolving basis that could continue indefinitely if all parties were in agreement. Of course there were always stacks of bases to visit in the South, some far more isolated than others, and the most boring parts were always going to be the bits in between visiting and playing the various chequered venues. This would usually involve an endless wait for jeeps, cargo planes or helicopters (either the large Chinooks or else the smaller Huey choppers) to ferry them to the next dot on the map where the troops would once again be thirsting for some live entertainment as a fleeting antidote to the mixed horror and boredom of war. The 300 dollars a show shared between them, after Horst Fascher's so-called deductions, wasn't really a fortune but as there was nothing much to spend it on anyway it was adequate. And in echoes of what he'd left behind, Tony would avoid the worst of the excesses that went on in Vietnam, although he would find that drugs were readily available in the combat area.

Question: *What about the incident involving Horst and the gambling?*

Reply (as told to the author/from notes made): The single most worrying incident outside of the obvious one of travelling around and the risk of getting themselves ambushed would occur when Horst, who always had a real empathy with the black troops, insisted on organising all-night gambling sessions and one day one of them would come close to ending in tragedy. Tony, who was on the outside looking in on this particular occasion, suspects that Horst had been systematically cheating his American opponents out of a considerable wad of dollars throughout one particularly long-drawn out night time gambling session before the inevitable happened and he was rumbled. The situation quickly turned from tense to downright nasty and Fascher was only saved from being severely injured, possibly killed, when Tony's German bass player Volker had the presence of mind to draw a gun and rescue his fellow countryman. Powerful stuff by the sound of it and one that TS remembers vividly to this day.

Whether it's related to the card-playing incident above or not isn't known but Horst didn't return with Tony and the group for the second stint in Vietnam after the Australian interlude but instead would opt to take on a somewhat cushier day job by operating a civilian agency in Saigon. But before that Australian time-out would arrive, and to their mass disbelief, Tony and his group would find themselves being honoured by the Americans hierarchy on the ground for the efforts they'd put in by entertaining the troops on the front line! He recalls this was to be a most bittersweet occasion by explaining that the Lieutenant Colonel who had orchestrated the awarding of their decorations was to be tragically killed himself soon afterwards, a human tragedy that TS recalls with deep sadness to this day. But on a lighter note the somewhat wackier element of the whole awards episode was that they more or less got to chose which rank or promotion they would receive! (More on this aspect shortly, but a bit more on Horst Fascher before we leave him.)

It seems Horst was someone who wasn't known for his charm and finesse back in Germany and had even served time in prison for manslaughter: but at least that meant that he was someone who could look after himself and the others if that became necessary. Interestingly Tony, when looking back and recalling their time together in Vietnam would actually say that he felt this whole Far Eastern episode probably saved Horst's life in a roundabout way, in that the latter was able to channel all his aggression into the equally demanding daily role of looking after his charges while at the same time sorting out the monetary side of things. Additionally, it was his responsibility to ensure that they got ferried to the next venue they were down to play. As to the money, this wasn't a fortune but then neither were their basic needs. With hindsight it's Tony's opinion that Horst, an inveterate gambler and wheeler-dealer, was creaming off some of the dollars that the group had to split between themselves, and getting whatever other kickbacks were being offered. But however unsatisfactory the whole thing became in monetary terms it was a price that had to be paid to keep the show on the road, although by the time the whole Vietnam bit was over TS hardly had a single dollar to his name. However it has to be added that he doesn't blame anybody as, whatever money he'd have got during this period, would doubtless been immediately spent in the nearest *PX or on some paid 'relief', if and when they occasionally hit somewhere that had any semblance of a nightlife.

**Footnote:* the name for a store in a United States military base which specialises in selling goods to military forces personnel.

Question: *You said that your adventures started even before you reached Vietnam. Can you explain please? (Note - It seems a hitch had arisen before the tour had even started, making their eventual arrival in Vietnam a hopelessly long-drawn out affair, as having initially arrived in the Far East they had first to be diverted north to Hong Kong and back. There they would find themselves enduring the whole web of bureaucracy that a war can foster before they could obtain the necessary visas and enter the Vietnam mainland.)*

Reply (as told to the author/from his notes) : It happened like this. On the plane ride to Hong Kong he vividly recalls sitting next to a soft-spoken and earnest young Vietnamese who he took to be a student and who proceeded to quiz him on every aspect of what he (Tony) was doing there and wanted to know just where his entourage would be going to while entertaining the troops. And for every question Tony answered it seemed another one would follow just as quickly. His questioner, who for some reason seemed intensely interested in the views and thoughts of a non-American musician, even persuaded him to write down some of his answers in the form of a report and Tony, who's never reticent to talk or put pen to paper when encouraged, readily acquiesced. It was only afterwards, when he and his group had finally disembarked in Saigon, that he was told that the man wasn't a student, but was probably an undercover officer in the Vietcong from the North!

With hindsight TS guiltily felt that he'd been far too forthright in expressing his political views to a total stranger but he was to become convinced in the months that followed that the word had been spread around that they were foreign musicians, and as such non-combatants who weren't to be targeted: in effect he's convinced to this day that his group received some modicum of protection during their stay. If that sounds fanciful it has to be said that they did live what was a pretty charmed life while over there, even if the time did come when it was reported that he was missing, presumed killed. But although the whole of the time spent in Vietnam was unremittingly harsh and dangerous at least he saw it through. He recalls a girl singer from Australia who'd arrived at the same time as his group and lasted just the one week before asking to go home. And back to Australia she was duly shipped without ever singing a single note!

Question: *And - as alluded to above - weren't you reported as killed or missing in action when in Vietnam?*

Reply (as told to the author/from his notes) : Although Tony has always been a prolific writer unfortunately no personal diaries or papers of his survive from this particularly chaotic period. And to fully reconstruct just what went on is well-nigh impossible although his fellow-travellers have vouched for the truth of much of what went on. Certainly it's known that during one of the annual Vietnamese Tet Offensives by the Vietcong (Tet is a three day Vietnamese festival which heralds in each lunar New Year) news reached the musical press back home that the singer Tony Sheridan was missing presumed killed in Vietnam whilst travelling through a military zone, and without having the protection that an armed convoy would provide. It was assumed that they'd made camp but were killed when their post had been overrun by Vietcong. Tragically, and to compound what was a dire situation, he admits that by then he'd been out of touch with his mother and step-father *"for several months"*, and they quite naturally began to fear the worst. Especially his mother, and his nearest brother Steve, even though he lacked having much empathy with Tony, even back then. (We'll come back to this 'killed in action' scenario when our story eventually reaches 1978).

Question: *I understand you all received honorary Army ranks when your initial tour of duty ended over there?*

Reply (as told to author/from his notes): Incredibly, they were all allowed to choose what 'decorations' they would get. Top of the list (and thus pulling rank) was Jimmy Doyle the drummer who decided he wanted to be an Honorary Major, while TS himself chose the rank of Captain and their bass player opted to be called Lieutenant Tondorff. Tony was to remain inordinately proud of the two bars which he would immediately have emblazoned on his cap although, unsurprisingly, they all had to take a lot of ribbing from any combatants they met up with from that moment onwards. And even stranger things were to happen during their return to Vietnam when they were given rocket launchers as weaponry to guard themselves against the possibility of an attack. Can you imagine that? Tony acknowledges that this whole period was *"craziness, but it* *happened."* But the plus side had been entertaining the troops and, in reminiscing about those days, he'd admit that *"it had been wonderful to be understood and also to be looked up to."* As mentioned, he's convinced that a film script could be worked up describing their time in Vietnam, something he still toys with trying to get off the ground. (Co-incidentally - but there's no connection with Sheridan - in the past year a film about the exploits of an Australian girl group during the Vietnam conflict has gone on general release, thus vindicating Tony's opinion from several years earlier.)

Question: *So what about that period in Australia which was sandwiched in-between the two tours in Vietnam? Was it at all memorable?*

Reply (as told to author/from his notes): There's not too much to say about the enforced interlude in Australia, which took place between those two tours, Tony mostly being holed up in Sydney on the East Coast. The original Vietnamese gigs having ground to a temporary halt about a year previous, all of the group needed some sort of period of rest, recuperation and one suspects even some female companionship. And the closest safety valve wasn't that far away in the shape of the Australian mainland to the south: where, in order to survive, Tony would find himself tapping into his country, skiffle and folk roots by playing in whatever bars in Sydney would offer him work. Money had also become so tight that as mentioned he even had to hold down a temporary 9 to 5 day job by working in a store, uniquely the only time he ever admits to turning his hand to paid employment, outside of music that is.

Tony is not particularly proud of this Australian sojourn for several reasons as he was really messed up at the time and remembers behaving quite badly even by his own lax standards of the day. For instance, he twice managed to get himself arrested and thrown into prison but, he insists, it was for nothing more outrageous than *"pissing in the street"*. Although a band member would embroider this by recalling having to get Sheridan out of gaol after he had peed on a cop's car with the officers still inside it! Whatever the true circumstances Tony feels that it was all a reaction to his time in Vietnam. He would go on to make a few Australia broadcasts and, as luck would have it, meet up with someone who'd become his new bass player, an Australian who went by the name of Leith, although his full name was Leith Ryan, and he it was who became the replacement for Volker Tonndorf for that second tour. Volker, at this point had decided he'd rather return to the safety-net of Germany than risk a further stint in the jungles of Vietnam. But however disruptive this whole period may have been Tony still had a life, and even a long forgotten English wife, their union having lasted some seven years and produced one child, to return to in his adopted homeland. And so the time would inevitably arrive, when he would head back to Germany and try yet again to put the pieces of his life back together. But it wasn't about to get any easier for the boy from Norwich for some time yet - a spiritual element was needed - badly...

Next Stop - Back to Germany

...chronologically our story has reached the onset of the Seventies but before turning the spotlight on the direction Tony's life was about to take it's a bit sobering to briefly contrast his life with that of The Beatles, given that a lifetime ago they'd all been thrown together in the musical German bubble that was Hamburg. But then, after this unique interlude had dissolved into history, it's well-documented that the Beatles had taken the musical world by storm leaving Tony behind in what appeared to be a European musical wasteland. To many that were weaned on the strains of American rock 'n' roll (including the author) it would seem that the Fab Four had achieved fame by simply playing a re-energised hybrid of rock 'n' roll and re-exporting it back from whence it came. But as we were soon to discover there was much more to the group than that superficial and rather simplistic view. Soon John and Paul would be veering down the path of singer-song writing (George too of course), creating even bigger headlines with their seminal Sgt. Pepper album and, almost at a stroke, leading pop music into all manner of new directions with the other groups languishing in their wake. As we now know a defining 20th century moment in popular culture was taking place before everybody's eyes. But alas for Tony there was to be no musical Sgt. Pepper moment at this particular juncture: for now his personal life remained fraught, while musically he'd also arrived at something approaching a crossroads. And it seemed, to all intents and purposes, that he'd turned his back on Britain for good…

CHAPTER 11: LIFE AFTER VIETNAM - A SAVIOUR APPEARS

"Just a few years ago all my life was a show,
I was always at the top of the bill,
I thought I was heading for the top
But I came to a stop now,
I was acting like the role I couldn't fill."

This Time. Composer - Tony Sheridan

BACK-STORY: We've already touched on Tony's early dabbling with transcendental meditation in Chapter 9 whilst he was in Hamburg, so we know that this relatively new form of religion (to most Western minds) was already part of his life. Soon it would take over his life completely, and at one point even side-lined his beloved music for a time. And we know that while the Beatles were giving full rein to their own involvement with these new spiritual movements by placing themselves at the feet of the Maharishi Mahesh Yogi at his ashram in India (1967/8), Sheridan was by then mired in the depths of Vietnam, where the search for the deep answers to life had to be temporarily put on hold. Of course he had a continuing inward struggle as religion, in its strictest sense, remained an anathema to him after his enforced contact with it during his school days as well as the abortive efforts his mother made to steer him towards the church. There had been little outward or cohesive thought on deeper issues whilst in Vietnam, although no doubt many of the events which he witnessed would be inwardly absorbed and would ultimately help to point him towards his life's path. With that thought in mind let's move on to more questions...

Question: *Before getting back to Tony's involvement with the Bhagwan Shree Rajneesh (mentioned in an earlier chapter) I needed to ask him some rather humdrum questions about life back in Hamburg. For example, he'd made some recordings in Hamburg under the name of Carole and Tony (circa 1972) - what was that all about?*

Reply (as told to the author/from his notes): After Vietnam life for Tony had taken on a more transient feeling and one he would liken to returning to Civvy Street, so totally had his life been affected by his stay in Vietnam amidst the American and Australian forces. He also had to face the fact that by now he'd left behind two failed marriages in his slipstream, had not seen much in the way of musical royalties at either and as far as the mainstream music business was concerned he'd largely fallen off the radar. The only thing to do therefore was to throw himself into his music wherever it led him: and soon life would become a kaleidoscopic blur that would find him at one moment in London and then as quickly back in Hamburg again. He accepted the fact that he couldn't expect to return to the music scene he'd vacated several years back as life had moved on for everybody, but fortunately yet another change of direction would soon present itself. It would probably be around 1972, when he was part of a European tour featuring a collection of visiting Americans, that fate would find him linking up both musically and otherwise with Carole Bell, one of a pair of twins from Liverpool, a city that has always been so pivotal a part of Tony's life. Carole, along with her twin sister Sue, and another sister Jean, had already had a minor career in the pop scene of the '60s, with some British releases on both Pye and Columbia, while calling themselves The

Three Bells. But these had never made much of an impact, and their career lacked any real breakthrough: hence they would find themselves like many others working on the continent.

Meeting up with Carole would lead the two of them getting up close and personal quite quickly musically speaking, and they'd eventually form themselves into a pretty successful Continental pop duo for a time, bringing with it a decided change of image as far as Tony was concerned. This would culminate in the Polydor release of a German single, as the duo Carole and Tony, entitled "Ich Glaub An Dich" ("I Believe in Love") coupled with the flip side, "Monday Morning". Issued in a gaudy colour sleeve, a novelty in those days, it portrayed the pair tastefully entwined and it did well enough in Europe, but it was never going to be anything other than an interlude in his life that would lead neither of them anywhere in the longer term. That said it was a period that would weave itself into another strand of Sheridan's colourful life, although musically speaking it could only be termed a dead-end however pleasant an interlude it was for a while.

Question: *Career-wise you moved in different directions as the 1970s unrolled didn't you? Acoustic music and also folk - I've also read you had a radio show for a time - how did that come about?*

Reply (as told to the author/from his notes): His life would certainly involve a lot of travelling in the coming years but even he can't remember the strict order of the various stopovers he made, as he was always looking for the next payday, the next gig, the next musical fix. For example it might mean a stay in Munich while, before long, he might be back in Britain again. This was followed by a sojourn in Hanover, only for Tony to return back to Hamburg yet again: the latter destination as often as not being sandwiched between yet more London visits. In all (and this has to be a real guesstimate) he would end up living in some eight different homes in as many different cities, albeit some stays over a six year period were much more fleeting than were others. In those days his luggage would consist of little more than a couple of cases, one full of books which he made sure followed him everywhere, while the other contained his personal effects and, in or out of its colourful case, his beloved guitar: long since fully paid for, and with those peccadillo's of his youth a thing of the past.

But his life desperately needed a prolonged period of stability at this point, and perhaps spending the whole of one particular year (1975) in Sweden, did introduce an element of permanence but not nearly enough to label his life conventional by most people's standards. He also recalls that somehow, despite seemingly always on the move, he still managed to DJ his own radio show over NDR2 (Nord-Deutsche Rundfunk 2) in Germany, a show which specialised in playing the American Blues music that was so dear to Tony's heart: *John Lee Hooker, *Memphis Slim, *Billy Boy Arnold and many other magical names were the staple fare. It was his choices that made the airwaves, and of course he has a speaking voice that could caress the listener and draw them in. It was a very different part of his life but a period he still remembers with some affection and even today he occasionally gets reminded about it when he bumps into a grateful listener from that distant past.

**Footnote:* One suspects these names were picked somewhat at random as, no doubt, Howlin' Wolf, Leadbelly or any of a whole host of blues greats could have been selected. Interestingly although most of the famous blues artists are long gone, Billy Boy Arnold (born in 1935) still performs as these notes were being typed.

Question: *With the author's notes becoming bewilderingly complex at this point I asked Tony to set down the next set of moves he made. With the pace quickening it will be seen, with hindsight, that a life-changing scenario was in the offing and he was about to take his involvement with the Bhagwan onto a whole new level.*

Reply (as told to the author/from his notes): After some head-scratching this is Tony's list of the various places he lived in during the course of the next eight to nine years:

1978/80 Los Angeles (USA)
1980/2 Hamburg (West Germany)
1982 onwards West Germany, India and Oregon, USA
1985/6 West Germany, Denmark and Italy
And thereafter back to the former West Germany

Breaking those countries down, we know from an earlier chapter that the time in Oregon refers to the attempt by the Bhagwan to move his Indian base there and set up a new Headquarters in the USA. Sadly, despite the concerted efforts of his many followers, it was not to be and it would all end in some disarray with the organisation forced to quit the New World, to avoid the Bhagwan's detention and possible trial. That was interesting enough for me to ask a follow up question and seek more answers.

Question: *What was the story behind that Oregon episode and the ignominious exit from the USA?*

Reply (as told to the author/from his notes): It seems that at the peak of his powers the Bhagwan's following was approaching a quarter of a million and, as Tony recalled, the step was then taken to relocate the movement's headquarters to Oregon in the process naming their ranch-like headquarters the Rajneeshpuram: a Buddha Field as the Bhagwan decreed it be called. The aim was to create a safe, secluded community centre, something which would have the power to expand and flower into something truly wonderful. Tony put his heart and soul into the transition, and the formation of this new community, as it was termed 'A New City for the New Man'. At the time of his arrival there Tony's attitude was, as he earnestly if savagely put it, *"fuck the music business"*. He was seeking to discover spiritual enlightenment and would do whatever it took to attain it.

Followers, who would be dressed in orange robes and sporting wooden beads, would sit at the feet of the Enlightened Master (the Bhagwan) and a dialogue would take place with his followers, an intensely spiritual time for those that partook. But sadly, that state was not to last too long and to say that Osho, the re-named Bhagwan, fell foul of the American authorities is to severely understate the case as at one time it seemed highly likely that he would come to trial on American soil. Instead the outcome was almost as draconian as, sometime during 1985, he was forcibly deported from the USA and his vision of a 'New City for the New Man', which had been started with so much optimism by his followers just a few years earlier, was effectively abandoned on a mass scale, although the movement would eventually regroup and remains in existence to this day, despite the Bhagwan's premature passing.

Question: *And the Los Angeles stopover deserves analysis as, following on from the death of Elvis Presley in 1977, Tony would head up his latter-day backing group, the TCB band, and together they would make a TV advertised album, and looked to be poised for opening in Vegas. What was that all about? (I was to learn that the story of Tony being 'missing in Vietnam' was dramatised and formed part of the album sleeve notes.)*

Reply (as told to the author/from his notes): The album, entitled World's Apart, had been recorded in Los Angeles with the active support of Elvis' *TCB band, who comprised a really luminous line-up. With Tony handling the vocals, his backing group comprised the wonderful James Burton on guitar, Glenn D. Hardin keyboards, Emory Gordy Junior on bass and Ronnie Tutt on drums: all are well-known to Elvis Presley fans and indeed to most of us who appreciate a certain style of music. Also helping out was Tony's Hamburg pal from the '60s, Klaus Voormann on bass, which was a welcome addition and someone who Tony could relate to. As to the music itself, one side of the vinyl album was deliberately Country in nature with a **Mickey Newbury number as well as "Lookin' Back" a Tony Sheridan original. Much of the remaining material featured more upbeat, rocking numbers such as "Rave On" and versions of Lloyd Price, Little Richard and Chuck Berry originals. All of the Americans backing Tony had absolutely superb musical pedigrees, whilst Voormann had become an in-demand instrumentalist himself back then, so what could possibly go wrong with such a stellar line-up?

**Footnote:* Standing for Taking Care of Business - the slogan so beloved of Elvis and his entourage.

***Footnote*: One of the greatest American singer-songwriters Mickey Newbury (1940-2002) is much missed. Although he recorded most of his own country-tinged songbook in his own unique style his talent was appreciated by his peers and all manner of artists have recorded his compositions, including Tony. Just the titles alone may convince you of his talent - "The Future's Not What It Used To Be" and "If I Ever Get To Houston (Look Me Down)" are just two of his many songs. Sadly he was not a recognised chart artist and never got the full recognition that he deserved.

Well, the album would turn out to be one of those US TV promotions that just didn't really click at the time. It was in fact briefly popular for a while, and if the whole thing had taken off as it should have, maybe Tony and the TCB band would have ended up as a Las Vegas act for years to come! And as mentioned the somewhat embroidered sleeve notes to the album would also include the story of how TS had been reported dead in Vietnam, but even exploiting that angle couldn't make the album a winner, although it remains a fine recording and one he remains proud of. (He played it to the author when I was staying in Seestermuhe with him). And, of course, as with this occasion he's always loved playing with first-rate musicians. But Tony was becoming increasingly unhappy during this whole American interlude and there is little doubt that he was still suffering from the after effects of his tortuous life and his time spent in touring Vietnam.

It's noticeable that Tony can soon self-destruct when he is being asked to do something that doesn't sit comfortably with him and here's how, years later, he would sum up that whole interlude in his life: *"I lived in California in 1978 and '79 and over there they look at you as something to market and project, and your feelings and personal life are ignored. It is like being a piece of meat. It is not my idea of being a musician."* Plainly he doesn't shed too many tears over that particular, abortive episode. As he put it he was very well paid, $600 a month, for being holed up in a Los Angeles motel for almost 12 months. Whatever the underlying reasons were the album didn't lift off like it should have done and so, after such a protracted period he was bursting to return to Europe and to try and pick up the threads of his life once again.

Question: *Tony's involvement with the Bhagwan and his movement has been total. He was asked more about this aspect of his life and asked how the commitment had affected his private life.*

Reply (as told to the author/from his notes): As we know earlier in his life Tony had briefly experimented with conventional Church routes which his mother had steered him towards back in Norwich but this had brought him little comfort, the only remote consolation being the access to the sacred music that such Church services might bring. But as far as he was concerned this was not nearly enough, and the Church of England framework back then and the pull from the pulpit of the Sunday sermons were for him frankly non-existent. When all of this is combined with his fractured childhood it really isn't such a big surprise that he would become alienated from such a conservative path and instead become attracted to one of the more fringe religions almost from the first moment that he'd come into contact with them. They offered a fresh, exciting way of life - seemingly the polar opposite of his view of existing religions - and the teachings of the Bhagwan were a shock to his system. As he put it they spoke directly to his heart.

Much of what has come to be written about the Bhagwan over the years makes him seem a controversial figure, certainly as far as outsiders are concerned, but nevertheless perhaps the Bhagwan holds the key to who Tony Sheridan really was back then and in fact who he largely remains to the present day. It was certainly at some indeterminate point during the 1970s that the life-changing philosophy of the Bhagwan Shree Rajneesh permanently entered Tony's life and, whilst still battling the demons that forever affected him, he decided that the time had come to do more than just read the Bhagwan's textbooks: he needed to immerse himself fully and live the life on a daily basis. Put like this it wasn't a decision that could be taken lightly. He would need to study rigorously to absorb the Bhagwan's teachings and this he would do over a long period until at last, on 12th March 1982, he became what is known as a Sannyasin. A momentous time in his life, and as he would forcibly put it to the author, *"life started again"*.

Symbolically, it seems that as a follower he had 'died' and been re-born. To fellow-converts he took the name of Prabu Sharan, of which the literal translation means "at the feet of God", a title he continues to cherish to this day. The teachings certainly had a major impact on the way in which he has led his life and the author can vividly remember Tony staying with him during the mid '80s while visiting Norwich for a school reunion. (I touched on this episode earlier.) At the time he had brought with him a book called When the Shoe Fits, a collection of 10 monologues given by the Bhagwan about the philosophies of the early Chinese Master Chuang Tzu. What was noticeable was that the book never left his side the whole weekend. He'd immersed himself in the

Bhagwan's teachings - those teachings, and of course, music were dominating his life and there was no middle course.

Question: *He was then asked whether his whole involvement with the Bhagwan affected just him or was his then wife involved. The author was aware from a local Norfolk newspaper article that Tony had a growing family by this time. Was that the case?*

Reply (as told to the author/from his notes): As we know from what has been said thus far travelling the world with little more than a guitar for a travelling companion didn't exactly help where family life was concerned. But his life and his religion had eventually all come together during the 1980s, when he acquired a new German wife Monika (also known as Arumina), and they decided to embark on the same religious journey together. Sadly Tony would later reflect with profound sorrow that *"possibly her heart was not in it"* although for many years he made a concerted effort to bring order and stability into his domestic life and as a team they would embrace the teachings of the Bhagwan Shree Rajneesh together. During the years that followed Tony and Monika (they had married in 1983) raised four children together and there must have been times along the way when it seemed his crazy life had finally entered into a period of prolonged calm. But sadly it wasn't to be, and eventually yet another painful break-up would come along and be made all the worse this time because of the involvement of a large and growing family. Although Tony will not discuss the break-up of this particular marriage - a marriage which lasted till the year 2000 - he is insistent that it was not his behaviour or actions that caused it - read into that whatever you will. But once again the pain of his past had seemingly caught up with him and one begins to wonder if he adopted the teachings of the Bhagwan because he had lacked a father-figure in his early upbringing? But it isn't the place of this book to seek to try and analyse my friend's life except in passing. There is no wish or intention of being in any way judgemental.

...it can be seen that the story of Tony's life thus far, through into the 1990s, has been quite detailed but over the remaining years there has not been too much to cast a spotlight on. He's been fully occupied making music and therefore, before our story ends, we need to look at his recorded legacy and see how that fits into his life and times. Certainly the author would urge anyone reading this work to seek out Tony's music, particularly the post-1960s stuff. It would be well worth doing so. (Towards the end of the book there is a section Recording Career - An Overview which may help the reader.)

CHAPTER 12: THE GRATEFUL EXILE - LIFE ON THE CONTINENT

"Now it's so much better as I got myself together,
Going to let you know how much it really means,
Just to laugh as a spectator,
Been an innovator,
When you know that nothing's really as it seems"

This Time. Composer - Tony Sheridan

BACK-STORY AND FINALE

Musically TS has remained consistently active over the years up to the present time although sadly his recording career has not always kept pace with his frequent in-person appearances and touring. It remains a depressing fact that despite consistently writing and performing his own original material, his catalogue is forever dominated by those Beatles-related re-issues, although they are occasionally coupled with some of the other stuff he did in Hamburg at that time. But the post '60s material is notoriously absent from his catalogue, certainly as far as the British record-buying public is concerned. There have been many musical highlights along the way none more so for TS than when, in 1995, he got to record in Nashville and the session would include Charlie McCoy, the harmonica player on several of Elvis' recordings, whilst the background vocals that day were provided by The Jordanaires, who surely need no introduction in these pages, and whose name was also often coupled with that of Elvis. And as if all of that wasn't enough, one of the songs recorded during that session was one of Tony's own compositions: *"That was a big thrill for me."*

As for touring he is simply much more selective these days but, usually in the company of a couple of South American musicians (one on bass, the other drums) he heads for Mexico, Scandinavia, Kazakstan or wherever else the feeling takes him and the promise of a paying gig awaits. A full run down of countries he's performed in and other projects undertaken over the years would fill many pages, but one suspects would be prohibitive to compile! In addition to the many venues throughout Europe and Scandinavia we mustn't overlook Spain and Italy, and the fact that he recorded an album in Milan during the '80s with his friend and fellow guitarist *Albert Lee. His official hand-out from a few years ago also indicated that he'd played himself in a German TV drama and a few years back he also made a musical DVD with the German singer Chantal when they were backed on stage by a classical orchestra. The moral gleaned seems to be that he follows his inner muse and goes wherever it may lead.

**Footnote:* Tony put me in touch with his friend and fellow guitar great to arrange an interview but we were unable to do other than exchange a brief e-mail circa 2007. What is certain is that over the years each has made flattering comments about the other's musical prowess. Co-incidentally an 18 year old Albert Lee would also make the pilgrimage to Hamburg in 1962 when, as a member of The Nightsounds instrumental group, he had the early thrill of appearing for a few weeks at the Top Ten club. (See Bibliography, Country Boy - a biography of Albert Lee which briefly makes mention of TS).

Needless to tell he's also played many Beatles-related events over the years, mostly one suspects either in Hamburg or Liverpool, while recalling his involvement with

Eddie Cochran he has also turned up at the annual Cheltenham memorial gigs. He's content to pursue a maverick approach to recording insisting to the author that, *"it must be right"*. In fact fairly recently he was enthusing about an album he was about to cut in Scandinavia only for the author to later learn that it subsequently hadn't happened. To which Tony's only cryptic comment was, *"Everything was not as it had seemed Alan"*. One suspects that life in and around Tony Sheridan will forever remain less than straightforward.

AND AN AFTERWORD

Musically speaking everybody the author spoke to in the writing of this book was unfailingly complimentary when asked to sum up what they thought about Sheridan's musical ability which makes his attitude in attempting to block this book all the more disappointing. The list of contacts the author approached included Ted 'Kingsize' Taylor, Albert Lee, Roy Young (although sadly in poor health as this was typed), Gerry Marsden, the late Dave Dee, Ray Ennis of The Swinging Blue Jeans, Dave Berry, Spencer Leigh, most of whom were spoken to whilst this project was originally being put together. The list is almost endless but has to remain selective. Many added further thoughts, in particular Gerry Marsden who apart from meeting and playing with Tony in Hamburg in the '60s also headlined a Las Vegas bill with him in 2007 and would thereafter recall, *"Tony was a great inspiration to both George Harrison and me when we were in Hamburg in the Sixties. Not only was he a great guitar player but he was a great singer too who had lots of charisma and a really great stage persona. He's a lovely lad and if anyone deserves to have a biography written about them it is Tony"*. A warmer tribute from a warmer man it would be hard to imagine.

Ted Taylor (remember Kingsize Taylor and the Dominoes?) who has also lived in Germany for years was particularly fulsome in his praise of Tony although most of his memories would have to be censored if they were to be published in a work such of this! Recalling that he did not see Tony after the '60s until a few years back the author asked him for his views. The reply?: *"it was the same old Tony, high, half pissed, older, and still a genius!"* But his admiration for Sheridan and his music remains unconditional and he is thanked for his thoughts. Dave Dee's principal memory was a particularly vivid one. He described the time when TS jumped over a Hamburg bar counter, followed closely by Dave, both managing to escape from the police who were coming in the Club via the front door. Dave Dee would then exclaim *"That's the last time I have a drink with you Sheridan, you're a dangerous man!"* But over and beyond that hair-raising memory he mostly talked of what a great musician Tony was: *"very bluesy"*. And what did the guitarist's guitarist (the legendary Albert Lee who we mentioned earlier) have to say? Out of a wealth of compliments we'll simply select a phrase he used that sums it all up, *"Tony Sheridan, he's my hero"*.

All of the above is positive. But let's leave the last word for now to a Hamburg contemporary and friend which also has the ring of truth: *"Sheridan? Do I remember Tony Sheridan? The man's a monster, a fucking monster!"* The speaker is Iain Campbell, the former bassist with The Big Six and believe it or not that quote, I'm sure, is meant as some sort of compliment! It only remains for me to say that my abiding aim throughout has been to avoid hi-jacking Tony's life-story or distorting it in any way. His life has been quite extraordinary and has needed little embellishment from me in the telling. But one final point in the believe-it-or-not category that the reader will just have to accept: Tony has never wanted anyone to overstep the mark and give himself any undue prominence in the story of The Beatles rise to super-stardom even though some individuals have occasionally tried to do so on his behalf. He acknowledges that he was caught up in something very special all those years ago and is grateful for the shared experiences that it brought him. He's adamant that the group would have achieved fame one way or another and that no one person or event should be thought of as the major catalyst. Certainly he played his part but so did very many others both before and after that epic Hamburg era. But, as the now Sir Paul McCartney has pointedly said about those times, *"We were baptised in Hamburg"* - and perhaps after reading much of what went on the reader will understand exactly what was meant by such a comment.

It's been said that in the history of rock 'n' roll Tony Sheridan was "lost in the shuffle". Maybe that's so, but let's just hope that at some point a few more will turn to his music and discover there's so much more to the man than as a minor footnote to a Beatles article. This may not have been the comprehensive biography that the author intended to write at the very outset but nevertheless let's hope it has managed to shine just a little light on a musical genius who has so often weaved his way in and out of my life over the years. As a song lyric might have put it, "I wouldn't have missed it for the world".

SELECTIVE BIBLIOGRAPHY

As to Beatles books there are far too many out there (probably 500+) to single out many for individual comment here although the group's own Anthology, in book-form and on video/DVD, were of great interest for obvious reasons even if, surprisingly, Tony Sheridan told the author that he wasn't formally approached for any input. Well that's what he said and instead he claims to be happy just to have got a passing mention. (In contrast he was a contributor to the excellent 1982 Compleat Beatles documentary, one of the first of its type, and of course has been featured in several other Beatles-related compilations down the years.) A few Beatles books are mentioned below but not that many as the present work makes no claim to be a scholarly one as far as the Beatles themselves are concerned, although they did impact heavily on Tony's life and, one would like to think, vice versa.

The other books featured below are a cross-section of those which the author consulted and all were felt to be of help in putting together the present work, none more so than the Gottfridsson and Krasker books. A handful of others were also felt to be essential, especially Pete Frame's The Restless Generation and a few years earlier Alan Clayson's Hamburg: The Cradle of British Rock; the latter providing a wealth of in depth information about the City of Hamburg while graphically describing the music scene there from 1960 and onwards. Sadly a large percentage of those listed below are likely to be out of print and all that the author can suggest is that readers search them out. Seek and ye shall find has always worked for me:

Anthology The BEATLES 2000 / Cassell

The A to Z of Buddy Holly and The Crickets Alan MANN 2009 / Music Mentor

Beatle! The Pete Best Story Pete BEST & Patrick DONCASTER 1985 / Plexus

The Beatles: From Fact to Fiction: 1960-1962 Eric KRASKER 2009 / Seguier

The Beatles - From Cavern to Star-Club Hans Olof GOTTFRIDSSON 1997 / Premium Publishing

The Beatles' Shadow: Stuart Sutcliffe Pauline SUTCLIFFE 2002 / Pan

Country Boy: A Biography of Albert Lee Derek WATTS 2008 / McFarland & Company

Don't Forget Me: The Eddie Cochran Story Julie MUNDY and Darrel HIGHAM 2000 / Mainstream

The Encyclopaedia of Beatles People Bill HARRY 1997 / Blandford

The Gospel According to The Beatles Steve TURNER 2006 / WJK Books

Hamburg: The Cradle of British Rock Alan CLAYSON 1997 / Sanctuary

Hit Bilanz: Deutsche Chart Singles 1956 - 1980 1998 / Taurus Press

Hit Parade Heroes Dave McATEER 1993 / Hamlyn

Mr Big - Ozzy, Sharon and My Life as the Godfather of Rock Don ARDEN 2004 / Robson Books

Ringo Starr Straight Man or Joker? Alan CLAYSON 1991 / Sidgwick and Jackson

Puttin' on the Style (The Lonnie Donegan Story) Spencer LEIGH 2003 / Finbarr International

Rock Family Trees Pete FRAME 1993 edition / Omnibus

Rockin' at the 2 I's Coffee Bar Andrew INGS 2010 / Bookguild
Skiffle Chas McDEVITT 1997 / Robson Books
Sweet Gene Vincent Steven MANDICH 2002 / Orange Syringe Publications
The Ultimate Beatles Encyclopaedia Bill HARRY 1992 / Virgin
The Walrus Was Ringo - 101 Beatles Myths Debunked Alan CLAYSON and Spencer LEIGH / 2003 Chrome Dreams

Several magazines, films and documentaries, etc were helpful when researching this work. Worthy of mention are:

"The Beatles with Tony Sheridan" 2003 DVD Universal Marketing Group GmbH. (TS was interviewed extensively for this documentary, which also features interviews with Horst Fascher, and many others from those Hamburg days. Much of the content is in German)

"The Beatles Anthology", Volumes 1 & 2. Video 1996 Apple Corps Ltd

"Backbeat" 1993 Channel Four Films production that recreates The Beatles Hamburg years. (TS is played by James Doherty, and briefly sings "My Bonnie").

The *Genesis* interview was given in 2002 and was sent to me by TS. It can still be found on-line at the time of going to print.

Now Dig This (edited by Trevor Cajiao) has been the UK's leading rock and roll magazine for a great many years and has been helpful when researching some of Tony's contemporaries such as Roy Young and others. *The Record Collector* is another magazine that comes up with nuggets of information having published a fine Sheridan Discography several years back. Recently a *Vintage Rock* magazine has made an appearance, published quarterly, and the January 2013 features the Beatles in Hamburg, where Sheridan gets a healthy mention.

Locally, The East Anglian Music Archive is run by Kingsley Harris and in 2013 they launch their new web-site. You should be able to find them located at: Musicfromtheeastzone.co.uk and Tony Sheridan's name will no doubt feature.

Finally Tony has had his own website for many years and this can be located by keying his name into your favourite internet search engine.

RECORDING CAREER - AN OVERVIEW

The listing which follows is highly selective and concentrates on Tony Sheridan's solo recording career, which has been ongoing, albeit intermittently, from 1961 through to the present time. Accordingly, it doesn't include those known recordings by others (Cherry Wainer, Vince Taylor and Brenda Lee for example) that Sheridan played on prior to migrating to Hamburg. It is hoped that this rudimentary listing will whet the appetite of the reader to seek out some of Sheridan's many other recordings, rather than just the Beatles-related ones that have been reissued ad nauseum since the 1960s.

GERMAN POLYDOR ALBUM RELEASES (unless otherwise stated)

Listed by year of release/album title/label - please note the format changed to CD in the '80s.

1963 My Bonnie — Polydor
1964 Just a Little Bit of Tony Sheridan — Polydor
1965 Meet the Beat — Polydor

(Note: Throughout the 1960s, 1970s and thereafter reissue and compilation albums of various permutations such as The Beatles First, Portrait of the Beatles, The Beatles in Hamburg, etc have appeared at regular intervals.)

1973 Tony Sheridan Rocks On!(Live in Berlin) — Metronome
1978 Worlds Apart — Antragon (released in the USA)
1984 Novus — MSP (released in Denmark)
1984 Tony Sheridan Volume 1 — Polydor
1984 Tony Sheridan Volume 2 — Polydor
1984 Tony Sheridan Volume 3 — Polydor
(all 3 above albums feature Sheridan's 1960 Polydor singles)
1987 Dawn Colours (with Albert Lee) — CGD (released in Italy)
1988 Here and Now — MSP (released in Denmark)
1997 Mother Earth Carry Me — New Earth
1999 Damals in Hamburg — Bear Family
2002 Vagabond — Bear Family
2004 Chantal Meets Tony Sheridan — Zounds (also issued on DVD)
2007 Tony Sheridan Live — WEMO

The chart career of the singer remains brief whichever category (single, extended play or long play album) is under the spotlight. In Britain the only Top 50 single listed is the 1963 issue of "My Bonnie", which charted the following year in the United States and led to the award of that Gold Record. It is estimated that the one million sales mark was reached during 1964. (The 45 rpm releases "Why"/"Cry For a Shadow" and "Ain't She Sweet"/"Nobody's Child" also made the American Top 100 Billboard charts during 1964.)

Surprisingly the only Sheridan singles that are listed in the German Top 10 charts throughout the years 1956 to 1980 both arose during 1964 when "Let's Slop" coupled with "Veedebook Slop Slop" reached No. 10 and "Skinny Minnie" c/w "Sweet Georgia Brown" got to No. 3 in an extended stay in the charts. "My Bonnie" wasn't a huge hit but did make the Top 40 charts in West Germany and also charted elsewhere in Europe. As to albums The Beatles Tapes album which charted in the UK during 1976 contained Beatles material from Hamburg but does not feature Tony Sheridan. A "My Bonnie" related album made the US Top 50 album charts in the 1960s - his only hit album in the United States.

APPENDIX 1: Astrid KIRCHHERR and the GERMAN CONNECTION

As to the constellation of German art students in Hamburg at that time, the principal ones have become well-known to many Beatles fans over the years, particularly the triumvirate of Astrid Kirchherr, Jurgen Vollmer and Klaus Voormann supplemented by the lesser known Reinhardt Wolff who also went on to become a photographer of note in later years. The term often used to describe this loose grouping of German artist friends has traditionally been that of 'Exis', or Existentialists, in its wider sense a 20th century philosophical movement, although the term is perhaps a misnomer when used in this context: another way was to talk about the artistic 'noir' scene of the day. But TS, an extremely artistic individual himself, has his own thoughts about the scene back then, particularly regarding the role of Astrid and her deep friendship with Stuart, although using the bland term 'friendship' in such a context seems hopelessly inadequate. Clearly the two were deeply in love and had already announced their engagement to their families and wedding plans being drawn up before the tragedy of his premature death intervened.

Tony was touched to see how protective Astrid was of Stuart and had talked about this aspect to Stuart Sutcliffe's sister Pauline. He said to her and repeated it to the author, *"She really looked after him. It was in a very violent place yet she managed to keep him a bit apart from the violence. I don't know how she did it, but she had a way of speaking to people that commanded respect from all types."* It was, he added, *"a very, very magical atmosphere in Hamburg at that time - and very important for the musical scene in Britain. We had a cocoon of very creative people involved with music and art and Stuart was a big part of that..."* If that smacks of pretentiousness his friend, Iain Campbell (of the Big Six) would cut through some of the mystique and use his own description of the German art students of the day when talking to the author. His more pithy description? *"Oh, that Arty Farty set!"* Tony when asked again about this whole scene remembers there being *"probably no more than 20 in the Hamburg 'noir' crowd"*, and in essence he felt that there was, in his words, *"not a lot of difference really from the Norwich Art School scene"*.

Voormann was to go on and learn the bass guitar (like Stu Sutcliffe) and have successful twin careers as both a musician (initially as part of Paddy, Klaus and Gibson in Britain, later as a member of the Lennon's Plastic Ono Band) and a separate career as a designer. Several of his many projects have linked him further with the Beatles over the years and Klaus would also turn his talents to record producing amongst other things as witness the 1978 Sheridan album World's End. Eventually things would come full circle for Klaus Voormann and his extraordinary love-affair with The Beatles when he worked on the artwork for the historic Beatles Anthology project in 1995. The remaining one of this unique threesome, Jurgen Vollmer, would also go on to carve out a successful career as a professional photographer and an example for pop fans was when his early photo of John Lennon was used as the iconic cover shot on the singer's 1975 album, Rock 'n' Roll. Of the main three individuals (Kirchherr, Voormann and Vollmer) mentioned above all, in recent years, have either written biographies or books that reflect on those Hamburg days, but these have not been listed in the abridged Bibliography of the present work.

APPENDIX 2: THE SAINTS SKIFFLE GROUP (1950s)

Before we finish it's also time to take a brief look at those youthful Saints who first got together as members of The Thorpe St Andrew Teenage Club way back when, and played their first gig at the Plumstead Village Hall outside Norwich when, it's said, their opening number would be "Don't You Rock Me Daddy O". True or not, as can be imagined their proficiency was no doubt pretty variable at the start but all had become hooked on the skiffle sounds they were hearing and their playing gradually improved. The principal members were, without doubt, its music-mad leader, Tony McGinnity, on vocals, guitar and violin, yes violin, backed by Andy Kinley drums, John Taylor on T-Chest bass and/or washboard, and Kenny Packwood, as the lead guitar. As to John Taylor, a quirky aside must be slipped in here, that John, a fellow retiree like the author, was discovered living on the south coast of England, in Southampton. That's a city whose football team just happens to have as its nickname, yes The Saints! Synchronicity, the friend of all authors whether they know it or not, strikes again.

Another occasional member from those days, and found to be still in Norwich (as at 2006) was Dougie Frost, who would replace the busy John Taylor in the group whenever the latter's sporting commitments intervened. Tony would remark: *"Dougie was a good drummer cum washboard player but he had eyes of different colours!"* Here again Tony's eye for spotting quirky personal characteristics comes to the fore. Given that he admits to being colour blind, one wonders whether the above remark is strictly accurate! As to Andy Kinley (who sadly passed away a few years ago) early pictures show him seated behind a solitary piece of drum equipment although he eventually acquired a full kit, a decided luxury for an amateur skiffle group of that time, when for most a washboard had to suffice to keep the tempo going. It also needs to be mentioned that The Saints had originally been put together jointly by Tony and another Club enthusiast, Vic Lowne, and the author was told tales of how they used to meet up in the latter's front room to practice: the daydream being that one day they would form some sort of band together.

Vic, who was known to all and sundry back then as Loon because of his abiding love of the '50s Goon show, played the guitar too, but he's the first to admit that he wasn't nearly as talented as his chum Tony. And so, when yet another even more talented guitarist joined in (that's Kenny above) Vic decided that the time had come to amicably step down and thereafter he'd set about forming his own group. Still an energetic and all round enthusiast to this day Vic would go on to form a rival outfit, The Kestrels. And in this brief round-up we mustn't forget either Mireille Gray and Alan Callf, both occasional members of the group, who were so helpful to the author when he was trying to find out about the early days back in Thorpe St Andrew.

And now a strange post-script. Norwich had its very own Liverpool Cavern in the form of The Orford Cellar situated in the heart of Norwich back then and Jimi Hendrix, Rod Stewart, David Bowie and Eric Clapton were among many musical legends who played there from the very early '60s onwards. But just as it was all beginning to happen there (and a Blue Plaque commemorating that dark and dingy venue hangs outside the premises these days) Tony and a selection of Saints were en route to the bright lights of London thus missing the chance to play there for ever.

APPENDIX 3: Tony's Early Groups

Readers will have realised by now that Tony Sheridan is a troubadour, or to borrow the title from his 2002 self-composed Bear Family CD, a musical Vagabond. And for the bulk of his life he has been content to be a strolling player who is happy to hand-pick two or more musicians to get himself the sound he wants for whatever gig or potential recording is on offer. Whether or not he's always been able to cherry-pick the best back-up musicians is probably unlikely as he does set himself and others very high musical standards. It also needs to be pointed out that before the decades on the road as a solo artist (and when he wasn't either following the Bhagwan or doing other things) his earliest years were always within a group structure: and usually as leader.

An over-simplified list of the various groups he either led or performed with during the late '50s or '60s are given below: while details of The Saints group can be found in Appendix No. 2 above. Please also note that there were many incarnations of the Beat Brothers during those days, and on occasions an attendant change in personnel.

1958/60 TS was a occasional singer at the 2 I's Coffee Bar, London.

1958/9 Vince Taylor and his Playboys: led by Vince Taylor on vocals.

1960 The Tony Sheridan Trio: "Oh Boy!" TV appearances, also as backing group to Conway Twitty, Freddy Cannon and others. Was also an integral part of the final Cochran/Vincent tour.

(to Hamburg, Germany 1960)

1960 The Jets: resident at the Kaiserkeller club.

1960 The Tony Sheridan Trio: resident at Studio X.

1961/62 Tony Sheridan and the Beat Brothers: Top Ten Club, etc.

Interregnum: 1961 recording sessions, Tony Sheridan and the Beat Brothers aka The Beatles, featuring Pete Best, George Harrison, Paul McCartney and John Lennon.

1962 The Tony Sheridan Quartet: resident at the Star Club from its opening in the April. Group featured Johnny Watson drums, Colin Melander on bass and Roy Young on piano and vocals.

1962/64 The Star Combo: included TS as leader, with, among others Ringo Starr on drums,

1964 Tony Sheridan and the Bobby Patrick Big Six: Top Ten Club

1964/66 Tony Sheridan and the Big Six. (Bobby Patrick having returned to Scotland).

1967 Tony Sheridan and the Beat Brothers once again, which by now included Volker Tonndorf who was to go to Vietnam with TS.

1968 onwards, TS was predominantly a solo artist

GLOSSARY

The select Glossary below concentrates on some of the individuals whose lives have either crossed with that of Tony Sheridan or who have influenced our hero, although it doesn't mean he necessarily admired all of them. And most certainly vice-versa! As an ageing rocker the author has primarily geared the list to the world of rock 'n' roll, while some other entries contain only the briefest of autobiographical information. It was not felt necessary to include John, Paul, George or Ringo.

Don ARDEN

One of a handful of impresarios from the '50s and one who employed TS although he was never actually Tony's manager. Had a flamboyant career, which involved managing acts as diverse as The Small Faces and his son-in-law Ozzy Osborne, while he also set up the Jet record label during the '70s. But before that he'd started off back in the late '40s as a singer/impersonator and even played the London Palladium. Later, he'd have an involvement with Hamburg and The Star Club - TS, who had known Arden since the 2 I's days would also meet up with him again in Germany. Don Arden described his life in an overly dramatised autobiography, Mr Big in 2002. Father of Sharon Osborne, he died in Los Angeles aged 81 in 2007, having suffered from Alzheimer's for some time.

Pete BEST

Not exactly the 'Fifth Beatle', Pete Best (born 1941 in Madras, India when it was still part of the British Empire) was quite literally the fourth Beatle for a while before he was unceremoniously sacked as their drummer just when they were poised for super-stardom. In his day an exceedingly handsome individual, it was said that he had his own Merseyside fan club back in the early Cavern days. Although leaving the Beatles caused him to become briefly suicidal he has gone on to carve out a long-term if low-key career in the music business. Several years ago he penned his musical autobiography (see Bibliography for details).

BHAGWAN SHREE RAGNEESH

It's probably best to stick to major reference books to research the Bhagwan Shree Rajneesh (1931-1990), the founder of the Neo-Sannyas Movement during the late '60s and a spiritual leader to thousands, rather than look elsewhere. But if you were to turn to a book on 'cults' that the author stumbled upon some emotive words start turning up: sex, drugs and mind-numbing meditation all being part of the movement's description. What is certain is that Bhagwan's early leadership led to meditation centres being formed in India, Europe and America and a sect was born that survives to this day, although by the time of the Bhagwan's passing he had taken the name Osho and that is how the organisation is now known. It can be seen that a simple footnote under this heading is quite inadequate to describe either the man or his teachings. For example the Bhagwan (literal translation = God) was born Rajneesh Chandra Mohan Jain but was also known as Acharya Rajneesh and by the time he had met a relatively early death both he and his movement were become known as Osho. TS remains a devout follower and will hear nothing against the movement: readers may care to investigate further and make up their own minds rather than accept a stereotype.

Joe BROWN

According to Joe Brown he could have ended up as Elmer Twitch if he'd have allowed Larry Parnes (see separate entry) to re-brand him: at least that's the famous quote that Joe has dined out on for years! But it has a ring of truth. A guitar genius who still tours night and day it can be assumed that he and Sheridan respected one another, having paid some heavyweight dues together when on that gruelling and ill-starred Cochran/Vincent tour back in 1960. Joe, forever a cockney to most of us, was actually born in Lincolnshire in 1941 and has not let his lengthy career stagnate having produced a musical output that has encompassed almost every musical style. His late wife (he has since remarried) also had a musical background and their daughter Sam Brown, a singer, has followed them into the business and has also had her own chart career.

Ray CHARLES

Ray Charles (1930-2004), who'd turned blind by age seven, is such a legendary artist that a few lines here are totally inadequate to do him justice. Little wonder then that his albums, even during his lifetime, include such titles as The Genius of Ray Charles while another used his name while adding, Living Legend to the title. Descriptions of the various musical genres he traversed include everything from pop to soul to jazz and country: and there's plenty of other categories although one should try to avoid such labelling. Frankly his voice could fit anywhere and he often proved it by dueting with any number of musical partners from Merle Haggard to Norah Jones. Not only are there many books about him but there was even a great movie, Ray starring Jamie Foxx (he won the Best Actor Oscar for his portrayal of Charles) made of his life which he oversaw in pre-production passing away a few months before its premiere.

Eddie COCHRAN

Edward Raymond Cochran was born on October 3rd, 1938 in the State of Minnesota, USA and, despite an all too short life, he has gone on to deservedly attain legendary status in the history of rock 'n' roll and its rockabilly offshoot. The fact that he was to die in an English hospital as a result of the injuries he sustained in a car accident near Chippenham, April, 1960, aged 21 would, like his friend Buddy Holly, sadly only help to cement his greatness. A superb guitarist, turned vocalist, he created a wonderful body of work during a very short time-frame, and we were to later find out that he'd appeared on countless other recordings as a session guitarist at Goldstar, a Los Angeles recording studio. He'd even found time to appear in several early rock 'n' roll movies, most famously a cameo part in the Cinemascope classic, The Girl Can't Help It with Tom Ewell and Jayne Mansfield. Overlooked in literary terms for years a biography, Don't Forget Me (see bibliography) finally appeared in 2000 and other books featuring Eddie - firstly by John Collis, and then one by Spencer Leigh - have followed in quick succession. Eddie is buried at Forest Lawn Memorial Park in Cypress, Los Angeles, California. The author has been to his graveside and seen the marker which touchingly shows Eddie holding his beloved Gretsch guitar. Is it any wonder that he always added underneath his autograph, surely with some form of presentiment, the legend "Don't Forget Me". Tony, a huge admirer of the singer's guitar prowess, was with Eddie during that legendary last UK tour and has often spoken movingly about those times. See also Glossary entry for Sharon Sheeley.

Dave DEE

To give him his real name of David Harman (1941-2009), Dave Dee is known to most music followers as the front man of the famous '60s pop act Dave Dee, Dozy, Beaky, Mick and Tich but anyone reading Alan Clayson's Hamburg: The Cradle of British Rock (see Bibliography) will know that Dave was in fact the leader of The Bostons who went over to Hamburg at around the same time as Sheridan. Another non-Liverpudlian, Dave and the rest of the group hailed from in and around the Salisbury area of England and they kept touring in '60s revival shows right up to Dave Dee succumbing to cancer. An illness he'd bravely battled for several years. A police cadet when in his teens he had the sad job of dealing with the aftermath of the 1960 car crash that fatally injured Eddie Cochran.

Lonnie DONEGAN

Lonnie Donegan (1931-2002) has to be looked upon as the founding father of Skiffle in Britain, and is certainly regarded as a musical lodestar as far as TS is concerned. Having an Irish mother and a Scottish father Lonnie (Anthony James Donegan was actually born in Glasgow) was for quite some time a featured member of the Chris Barber Jazz Band until he recorded "Rock Island Line" and the rest, figuratively and literally speaking, is history. Not only did that record reach the Top Ten in the UK charts in January of 1956 but it actually transported itself into the US Billboard pop charts, where it peaked at No.8, a very rare occurrence back in the '50s. Although Lonnie's name is synonymous with skiffle most fans will appreciate that he could perform in many varied genres, having at one point made comedy recordings alongside Max Miller, while also taking a ballad ("The Party's Over") into the UK charts during the early '60s. You could never keep a good man down and, although having confronted major health problems for a period of years, he continued to perform until the road ran out and he collapsed whilst mid-tour, dying soon after being hospitalised. A 2003 biography by Spencer Leigh, Puttin' on the Style, (see Bibliography) sensibly concentrated on the singer's musical legacy rather than his somewhat convoluted private life.

Vince EAGER

Anyone reading Tony's story will know that Vince, who was born Roy Taylor in Grantham back in 1940, was not Tony Sheridan's best buddy. One assumes there's a mutual antipathy which leads back to those 2 I's and touring days of the '50s. However, Eager has enjoyed a prolific career that has endured despite the fact that he never actually had one single UK chart hit although he has had a slew of releases via the Decca, Parlophone and Top Rank labels. Still performing as of this writing he has also penned a book of anecdotes under the heading of Vince Eager's Rock 'n' Roll Files. More power to his elbow - at least he continues to fly the flag for rock 'n' roll. It's surely possible to come from Grantham, Norwich or almost anywhere and still sing rock 'n' roll if the feeling is there.

Horst FASCHER

The name of Horst Fascher (born 1936 in Hamburg) is synonymous with the music scene that Sheridan inhabited in the early '60s. It's a curious coincidence that 2 of the individuals that got the 2 I's up and running in London had a wrestling background whereas a counterpart in Germany (Fascher) was a former featherweight boxer! Read up on Beatles lore during those formative years and many lurid stories abound of what was undoubtedly tough grounding for all concerned. Horst was involved with both the Kaiserkeller and the Top Ten Clubs and, of course, was to travel to Vietnam with TS, before eventually making his way back to Hamburg. According to Bill Harry's Beatles People Encyclopaedia (see Bibliography) Fascher has led a life dogged with tragedy.

Henry HENROID

Henry Henroid (1936-1998) was, in the words of the Beatles chronicler Bill Harry (see Bibliography), one of the true unsung heroes of the British rock 'n' roll scene going back to the '50s and '60s. An agent, a manager, it's hard to put an exact label on the man. But his name is interwoven throughout the era and, for example, it was he who first spotted The Animals and contacted Mickie Most leading directly to their being signed up for their first big recording contract. He also had the almost impossible task of trying to manage Gene Vincent at one point: and it can be seen from talking to Tony Sheridan that TS retains very fond memories of the man. Sadly Henry developed a debilitating illness and died before his time. Bill Harry would write a fulsome tribute to him for his Mersey Beat publication.

HODGES Chas

Not easy to pen just a few lines about such a versatile individual as Chas Hodges, piano player extraordinaire who, together with his musical partner and guitarist Dave Peacock, have become almost a musical institution over the years under their collective name of Chas and Dave. They had almost a decade of UK chart hits spanning the '70s and '80s with their so-called 'rockney' styled music - a unique fusion of cockney and rock - and have a tour lined up for 2013 even as this is being penned. But Chas in particular has a musical pedigree that goes back further to his days in the '60s as a Tornado when he played bass on the group's worldwide hit "Telstar" (see also the Joe MEEK glossary entry), and years later would also appear in the biographical movie of the same name Telstar. He was also a member of the Outlaws (another Meek-related group) who backed Mike Berry and in latter years has teamed up with Crickets drummer Jerry Allison to record a superb album in Nashville. Born in Edmonton, London in 1943 you can visit the Chas and Dave official web-site to find out more, or read his autobiography (styled Chas and Dave: All About Us) which came out in 2008 complete with a parental advisory warning on its cover!

Buddy HOLLY

The late Charles Hardin Holley, Buddy Holly to you and me, was all too often labelled a Tex-Mex singer, because his roots lay in West Texas with Mexico just across the border and New Mexico even closer. A hugely influential '50s artist the connections with TS are too numerous to list fully here, although their actual paths were never to cross. Tony was a huge fan from the very start and (for example) would eventually sing "Oh Boy!", the big Crickets hit, live on the similarly named British TV show of the '50s: in the '70s he'd get to record a Holly/Crickets hit with "Rave On" forming part of his Worlds Apart album which he made with the TCB band. To this day Tony sings "Not Fade Away" as part of his live set, more than often as a finale. His admiration for Holly is immense as anyone reading the present work will have realised by now. Buddy Holly is one of only a select handful of singers from the 1950s who still has total street credibility and whose music, via his unique recorded legacy, still lives on in the 21st century. He was born in September 1936 in Lubbock, Texas and was killed in a plane crash while part-way through a tour of the American Midwest in February, 1959. The crash (eulogised as the Day the Music Died) would also claim the lives of the Big Bopper, Ritchie Valens and the young pilot Roger Peterson.

Joe MEEK

Don't read this brief Glossary note to learn about the incredible genius of pop producer Joe Meek (1929-1967): instead, read the definitive biography of the man by John Repsch or else watch the more recent dramatised film of his life entitled Telstar. Both give a glimpse inside his tortured life (Repsch was in fact a consultant on the film) although the whole story of his life is almost impossible to encapsulate and fresh discoveries about his life and musical legend continue to this day. There's also an excellent active Joe Meek Society that honours his memory and puts out an excellent fanzine, Thunderbolt - search it out. If you didn't know, probably his greatest work involved instrumentals and, of course, "Telstar" the worldwide 1962 hit by The Tornados, is probably the best known of all his works. It's remarkable to think that he didn't come from a known musical background and was brought up in rural Newent, in Gloucester travelling to London like many others in the '50s. Belatedly recognised as a true musical genius, he was light years ahead of his time.

Mickie MOST

Much missed pop singer turned pop mogul whose main chart success as a performer was in South Africa during the late '50s when he made a practice of covering Buddy Holly hits. He had only one minor hit in his home country and was actually born Michael Hayes in 1938 in Aldershot and acquired his more pop-sounding persona of Mickie Most in 1959: incidentally at almost exactly the same time as TS adopted the name of Sheridan. A forward thinking individual Mickie amassed a financial fortune from his various business interest but is most famous for producing the work of The Animals, Lulu, Herman's Hermits, Suzi Quatro and a host of others. He died from a cancer-related illness in 2003.

Larry PARNES

Lawrence Maurice Parnes (1930-1989), in his prime his palatial home had a doormat with the initials LMP emblazoned thereon, was certainly at one point the best known British pop impresario and in the '50s built up a legendary stable of talent, the majority of whom he endowed with hip-sounding names, even if today it all sounds somewhat quaint. Fury, Eager, Power, Wilde, Fame, Fortune, Gentle the names could almost take over this Glossary if we were to let it. But humour aside he did have the Midas touch and no doubt many individuals have a lot to thank him for. Not only did he guide careers but he set up many a pop package in the late '50s and early '60s. His enterprise would wind down over the years and he died somewhat early aged 59. The US Billboard music bible would strikingly say by way of eulogy, "Larry Parnes' stable of artists changed forever the face and sound of UK pop".

Sharon SHEELEY

The name of the Los Angeles songwriter Sharon Sheeley (1940-2002) is forever linked with that of Eddie Cochran: most famously as the girl-friend of the late singer for whom she wrote the classic "Somethin' Else". She was in Britain with Eddie throughout that fateful 1960 tour and was also a passenger in the speeding car which would crash en route to the airport, killing Cochran and badly injuring his co-star Gene Vincent. Sheeley composed a handful of classic pop songs in the late '50s and early '60s, some in her sole name, while for a time she also co-wrote material with her friend, the singer-songwriter Jackie De Shannon. By far their most famous composition was "Poor Little Fool" a US No.1 for Ricky Nelson in 1958. Among others Sheeley also wrote songs for The Fleetwoods, Ritchie Valens and Eddie Cochran during her those years but her career would wane during the 1960s, and she later left the mainstream music business.

Tommy STEELE and Colin HICKS

Tommy Steele (who was born Thomas Hicks in 1936, but given his more familiar name by Larry Parnes - below) was probably Britain's first big rock 'n' roll star who would, for a short time, also become a matinee film star. It was a wonderful launching pad to morph into one of the country's greatest all-round entertainers and he's still box office to this day, starring in the West End of London as Fagin in Oliver as this is being typed. Sadly his younger brother, Colin Hicks (born 1941) never quite made the same breakthrough and was always a lesser light in his home country. But he did have a reasonably successful '50s pop career as Colin Hicks and the Cabin Boys that saw him have several record releases albeit nothing charted. He took himself to the Continent and to Italy in particular, where for a time he became quite a big star, and appeared in a film. But he hasn't been heard from much in recent years musically speaking but is still to be found doing the occasional rock 'n' roll weekender event.

Stuart SUTCLIFFE

As can be guessed from the name, Stuart Fergusson Victor Sutcliffe (1940-1962) was born in Edinburgh and spent most of his adolescence in either Scotland or Lancashire in the north of England before moving to Liverpool and Beatles territory. It was there as a 16 year old that he met up with John Lennon at Art College and they formed a rare bond. It's very clear that Stuart was an extremely talented artist but seemingly much less proficient on the guitar. But he had acquired a Hofner President bass guitar and for a while looked every part the mean and moody member of the early Beatles as a whole portfolio of photographs from those Hamburg days demonstrate. Turning more and more to art to the exclusion of music he tragically died of a bleed to the brain at age 21 before he had had time to fully exploit his artistic talents. Of course, his artwork is highly collectable to this day and has often been exhibited over the years.

Vince TAYLOR

Vince Taylor (1939-1991) was actually born Maurice Holden in London before moving to the USA as a teenager. When the rock 'n' roll era burst forth in America he opted to try and hop aboard the boom in his birth country rather than in his adopted American home. So the rather extraordinary situation arose whereby, Vince Taylor as he was now called, arrived back in Britain complete with a US manager, set to conquer us Limeys! He was spotted at The 2 I's, along with Sheridan, and as Vince Taylor and the Playboys they held down a resident spot on the "Oh Boy!" TV show. As we know TS, as a member of The Playboys, backed him on both the TV shows and also on one of his Parlophone releases. Rather like Vince Eager he was very popular as a live act but that success failed to translate itself into a single hit record. He was also seen by many as a leather-clad Gene Vincent clone. With success hard to sustain in the UK he had a reasonably successful career in France for a while but drug and alcohol problems may have contributed to his early cancer-related death at age 52.

2 I's COFFEE BAR

The legendary venue (it was at 59, Old Compton Street London in the heart of Soho) for so many rock 'n' roll wanabees who began swarming there from 1956 onwards when Tommy Steele first brought it into the outer reaches of the nation's consciousness. Thereafter many hopefuls would follow in his footsteps including Tony Sheridan. The music itself actually took place in a rather dark overcrowded basement area: but the beauty of things was that almost anyone with an instrument could turn up and within days find themselves trying out on it's makeshift stage. The story of the venue would eventually be told fully with the publication of the Rockin' at the 2 I's Coffee Bar book (see Bibliography) whereby every short chapter is a separate reminiscence by artists who performed there. Sheridan gets many a mention, but dare it be said not always that favourably!

Gene VINCENT

In Britain and France, Vincent Eugene Craddock (1935-1971) from Virginia, USA, is probably the most revered of all hard-core rock 'n' roll performers yet, in his own country, he would have just the one Top 10 recording and that was his first, back in 1956. Even as early as late 1957 his recording career back home was as good as over and it was to Europe that Gene headed with very mixed results. But he's left behind a wonderful legacy of recordings, mostly via the Capitol label, although many others (on Challenge, Dandelion, Buddah/Kama Sutra, Rollin' Rock, etc) are well worth seeking out, containing diverse material ranging from classic rock 'n' roll to ballads, country, folk and even soul ("Bring It On Home"). There's even a classic put-down to his manager, Don Arden contained within his version of "Our Souls" - a play on words if you're wondering exactly what. Think about it! Of course, Gene died much too early of bleeding ulcers aged 36, and is buried in the Eternal Valley Memorial Park, in Clarita, California. Tony would first encounter Vincent along with Eddie during that famous last 1960 UK tour that ended so tragically. Although Eddie Cochran was gone TS would link up with Gene several times as he explains in detail in the present book.

Cherry WAINER

Like Tony for a time, Cherry was a resident on the '50s TV show "Oh Boy!" where she both played the organ as a solo act, while at other times she was featured as part of Lord Rockingham's X1. That Harry Robinson led instrumental group are fondly remembered and had several great UK instrumental hits most famously the 1958 No.1 "Hoots Mon!". Although she never charted as a soloist she covered Dave "Baby" Cortez' 1959 US No.1 "The Happy Organ" for the British market but it surprisingly failed to make the charts here, as did the Cortez version. As mentioned in the text TS played guitar on this session although, in line with the normal industry practice, he wasn't credited on the label. Reference books say Cherry Wainer was an honours graduate of the British Miles of Smiles Academy and there were hopes she would become the female Liberace, the famous glittering pianist of that era. But her career tailed away, and later details are not known.

ROY YOUNG

One of only a handful of British singers from the '50s who could sing rock 'n' roll with any conviction and readers of a certain age will still remember him from Drumbeat (BBC TV) days, standing at the piano (shades of Little Richard) while pounding out his frenetic version of Larry Williams "She Says Yeah". Sadly, as with Vince Eager he didn't find his way into the British charts of the day, so he too eventually made the trek over to Hamburg where, for most of the 1960s, he found work in the clubs around the Reeperbahn district. When in Germany he would often back TS on stage and also appears on many of Tony's Polydor recordings from that era although, it must be noted, he was not involved in all of the "My Bonnie" sessions - very few of the tracks feature any piano. Like Tony, Roy is now in his 70s and he trod a path from the wiles of Oxfordshire to London seeking fame and fortune at the musical Mecca which was the 2 I's. As can be imagined has a lengthy musical pedigree from those '50s Drumbeat (TV) days, to being part of Cliff Bennett's superb outfit, to operating his own group The Roy Young Band for many years. Famously appeared on stage with The Beatles in Hamburg during the '60s, and was on many other recording sessions back then. Like Tony Sheridan has lived most of his life outside of these shores which includes many years based in Canada. Contributed several lengthy interview segments to the DVD documentary, The Beatles with Tony Sheridan.

ACKNOWLEDGEMENTS

This list has been kept fairly brief and the author offers a blanket apology to any name that he has accidentally overlooked. The list includes both friends from my schooldays who knew Tony McGinnity (aka Sheridan) in all his manic glory and a collection of several others who have given encouragement or tangible help during the book's long drawn out gestation. But further apologies are necessary in that many of the anecdotes and stories related by several of those named below have not been used: they would fall victim to the major revision of the text that the author has been obliged to carry out in order to bring the book to publication.

Nevertheless, those who offered to help are listed alphabetically below: Barry Allard, Bruce Austin, the late Alan Callf, the late Dave Dee, the late Evelyn Elliott, Annetta Evans, Peter Feast, Mike Flowerday, Nick and Lavinia Ganley, Lawrence Guymer and Stacey, Stephen Guymer, Trevor Hardy, Kingsley Harris of the East Anglian Music Archive, Ray Hollands, David Howard, David Hunt, Ken Hustler, Derek James of Archant, Spencer Leigh, Macca who I tried desperately hard to contact without success, Gerry Marsden who delightfully did get back to me, David and Jane Mesmer, Roger Parsley, Simon and Susie Pritchard, John Sendall, Tony's son Tony Sheridan junior in Florida, Wayne Smith, Peter Steward (to whom the book is dedicated), Martyn Street, John Taylor, Kingsize Taylor, Nicky 'Buddy' Walker, Ian Westgate, Barry and Penny Whiting and Trevor Whitworth. I must also include my stalwart friends in Florida and Las Vegas namely Bob and Sue Dees, Howard and Mary Olson and Jerry and Kathy Zapata - it shows the lengthy gestation period that this book has undergone that sadly three of those same friends are no longer with us. Almost at the end, I must not overlook my son Richard and thank him for the protracted loan of his Beatles books and his wife Jane Penrose for her many publishing tips. But sorry Jane if I haven't used too many of them! And of course, my wonderful wife Pam who has lived through the trauma of her husband producing yet another book. But at least it has hardly any mentions of Buddy Holly!

Grateful thanks are given to my usual publisher George Groom-White of Music Mentor Books who was working on the original manuscript when the plug was pulled. He graciously withdrew from the project without any recriminations - one heck of a gesture. What now remains is basically all my own work but certainly a lot poorer without George's input and attention to detail. Despite the difficulties in getting this book out Tony and his late wife Anna Sheridan in Seestermuhe, Hamburg are thanked unreservedly. They have tolerated and perhaps occasionally enjoyed my repeated intrusions into their lives and Tony has always tried to co-operate manfully with my assorted questions even when I've clearly antagonised him. Mind you I have occasionally bribed him with precious presents from our shared schooldays such as an Old Boys scarf as well as several CNS school yearbooks. I've stopped at nothing to extract details of his incredibly convoluted life but somehow I still think there's much more to tell *("Alan my private life is sacrosanct")*. And it must be emphasised that although Tony provided a wealth of quotes which I've used extensively he did not have any editorial control over what finally ended up in the book. If there is any misrepresentation I am extremely sorry and can only say that it's been totally unintentional and hopefully has not jeopardised a friendship which I trust is ongoing. Hopefully it will in fact have boosted his career - I can but hope.

A Sad Postscript

Anna Sheridan (Tony's wife) passed away at the young age of 34 in 2011. When I started this book I envisaged a happy ending for them both - Tony had finally found what he was looking for in Anna (they were to marry in 2005) who was the most loving person and supported him in everything he did from the time they first met up when, as a fan, she went to see him sing. He told me that he never expected to marry or find happiness again but he did, although this was to be tragically short-lived in earthly years. Both would find themselves battling cancer and in March 2008 Tony had to have his left kidney removed. For Anna her cancer was to return and she died on 10th September, 2011. She was wise beyond her years and I well remember my first meeting with her at a CNS reunion in 2006 when Anna accompanied him on his trip to his birth-place. Talking with him later that evening I indiscreetly asked Tony how old Anna was: he replied that she was a wise soul, who was three thousand years old! And, by the way, he really truly meant it. He had found an intense happiness, and how sad it was that it wouldn't last. My memories of having met Anna are nothing but happy ones. R.I.P.

"Looking back - it almost makes me cry a little
Even though I'm not a sentimental man
Don't you ever despair, we'll make it if we dare,
Make it this time for sure".

This Time. Composer - Tony Sheridan

END